SOUNDINGS

*for David Henderson,
my friend,
Bill Heyen
June, 2008*

Praise for *Soundings*

"From corporate plots over beers at the Wynkoop to scandal in the Tech Center, Charland's *Soundings* exudes the real Denver—and few protagonists offer such a clear-eyed view of a corporate world gone whacko as Hawk Kidree, an ink-stained wretch of a hero with one foot in flackdom and the other up the bad guy's ass."

> Tom Schilling, CEO, *Intermountain Corporate Affairs*

"*Soundings* cleverly 'peeks' (read the story and you'll get it) into Denver's high-tech buzz and corporate downsizing, through a lens of enticing relationships and sly business transactions that go awry. Charland's sharp pen offers an intriguing read."

> Rich Feller, Professor, Colorado State University, and coauthor of Knowledge Nomads and the Nervously Employed

"Bill Charland has captured the go-go years in Denver with *Soundings*. The characters are appealing, and his knowledge and affection for the city are apparent."

> Jon Talton, author of the David Mapstone mysteries, including Arizona Dreams

"In the great American tradition of Enron, WorldCom, and Tyco comes Bill Charland's fascinating tale of greed, hubris, and corporate folly. *Soundings* takes us back to a world looking the other way while the harbingers of today's heinous corporate scandals and collapses were first flitting across the radar. I couldn't put it down."

> David Van Meter, author of Body of Evidence *and* Necessary Evil

SOUNDINGS
WILLIAM CHARLAND

Soundings

Copyright © 2008 William Charland. All rights reserved. No part of this book may be reproduced or retransmitted in any form or by any means without the written permission of the publisher.

Published by Wheatmark™
610 East Delano Street, Suite 104
Tucson, Arizona 85705 U.S.A.
www.wheatmark.com

International Standard Book Number: 978-1-58736-878-3
Library of Congress Control Number: 2007930007

for David Van Meter

and George Stein

This is a work of fiction. All names and characters are either invented or used fictitiously. The events described are mostly imaginary, except for individuals who are mentioned by name.

1

If you were to ask him how it all began, Hawk might tell you of a time in Denver, back in 1995, early in September. It was an ominous night, as the sun sank low behind the foothills and the clouds began to fire up in burnt orange and magenta.

It was a hallowed night in Denver: the start of football season. The clouds were monstrous—jet stream high and cumulous—and they appeared to pack plenty of snow. Sitting in his Subaru, he breathed a sigh of gratitude for all-wheel drive, and continued to marvel at the sky. It was either that or stare at a freeway crammed with 60,000 football fans, creeping toward Mile High Stadium on an asphalt track that was clogging like a fat man's arteries.

It was the first Monday night game of a 1995 NFL season that had Super Bowl possibilities for the Denver fanatics. The Broncos were already 3 - 0, and this game would be a showcase for both the team and the city that fancied itself the center of all things cultural and technological in the Rocky Mountain West.

Now, what if it snowed? The clouds that were hovering over the ski resorts could just as easily slalom down to the stadium. Which made for interesting imagery. There was nothing like a blizzard on network TV to convince the rest of the nation that Denver was a nothing but a backwater outpost for mountain men who sat around and guzzled Coors all day.

The traffic came to a standstill just beyond the parking lot, and that's when he saw it. He'd been gazing up at the

Denver skyline—just a few, scant skyscrapers looming over a downtown he could walk across in twenty minutes. But the buildings were stunning, sparkling in the last rays of the fading sun. On the top floor of the tallest, an enormous neon sign spelled out the biggest employer in town, Telwest.

Your Future at the Speed of Light. He remembered running the focus group where someone had come up with that tagline. Telwest: once a stodgy, public utility, but nowadays a happening place in a deregulated industry, some would say. Purveyor of some glitzy new talk-toys. From POTS to PANS, the saying went: plain old telephone service to pretty amazing new stuff. It was said the video phone was almost ready for market. And that was just the beginning. One day, there'd be nothing less than three-dimensional television.

Telwest: guarantor of 60,000 jobs, enough to fill the Broncos' stadium. The sign was a monument, in blazing blue, to the largest corporation in the time zone. It was said you could see a blur of neon blue all the way to Wyoming.

Finally he drove up to the parking lot attendant and turned his attention to terra firma. But as he fumbled with his wallet, something in the rearview mirror caught his eye. At first he blinked and shook his head. But no. It seemed the big, blue sign had begun to flicker. One letter at a time was going dark. As he passed through the gate, he looked back once more.

Now the skyline of Denver was a black void. He felt a sudden chill and shuddered. His one and only client worked for that corporation. For an instant, he had a shivering sense that Telwest was no more.

The next morning, the alarm beeped at 7:30, and he opened one eye to a shaft of bright light that beamed across his bedroom from beneath the window shade. He squinted his way to the window and flipped the shade.

Seven stories below his high-rise condominium,

Cheesman Park sparkled with a patina of new snow. As always, in Denver, the snow was both a curse and a blessing. By noon, there'd be a floodtide of slush to contend with as the temperature climbed to fifty degrees. But for now, the world looked fresh and new—almost virginal.

He wondered if this were a vision he might carry through the day: primal Colorado. Just the mountains and the plains, before all of the... He tried to stop. This was no way to start the day. Why was he always sifting through Denver, searching for something beneath it?

He switched on the television and watched the blizzard once again. Cynically, he thought the timing could not have been better. A Broncos game in a snowstorm on national TV meant the flow of immigrants slowed a little.

As he padded around the kitchen making coffee, he glanced at the replays now and then. There was John Elway, trotting out to the huddle in fresh cleats as the snow came billowing over the foothills. The Broncos had been privy to an up-to-date weather report at halftime, and they'd changed their shoes. The Atlanta Falcons, it seemed, had not.

The touchdown that decided the game had come early in the third quarter, as the Atlanta defensive backs slipped and slid like snowboarders. Fast forward to Elway, setting up to throw from the Falcons' forty-yard line. Benjie Green, his favorite receiver, juking his defender with a hip fake at the twenty, then racing into the end zone as Elway hit him in stride.

The camera panned to the hapless Falcon defensive back, sprawled face first in a snowdrift. Then it swooped up to capture the orange-clad crowd, swaddled in their parkas, roaring shoulder to shoulder in the teeth of the storm.

He gave a wry smile as he switched off the television. Denver would be fun today. That was always the way when the Broncos won. The city would go ecstatic. So, why couldn't he join in, feel a part of it? He lumbered into the bathroom and turned on the shower. With a glance at in the mirror, all the Saturdays of football came rushing back to him.

At 6'4 and 250, he was close to his playing weight. If you didn't count the gristle that was starting to gather like croissant rolls around his midriff. He closed his eyes and listened to the blare of brass bands and the crowds. He remembered the headlines: Hawk Kidree Dominates at Offensive Tackle. Kansas' Kidree Named All Big 8. Then the last lead story on the sports page: Kidree opts out of senior year. Walks off the team. Tells reporter he's serious about journalism major, wants to "concentrate on his studies."

There were those in Denver who remembered Hawk Kidree, the football star, and he tried to avoid them. Some still thought of him as an Indian sports legend. Hawk thought about his "date" last night, to use the term loosely. What was her name? He thought for a moment but couldn't remember.

She was a slim woman with a nice-looking face framed in rimless granny glasses. She might have been an interesting person to get to know; there was a studious look about her. But those glasses! It had been your basic bar encounter, after the game, in one of those renovated, fern-and-ficus, warehouse saloons that had sprung up all around the stadium.

A brew and a screw back at her place. He recalled how quickly she had stripped and jumped into bed. He wondered why: she wasn't all *that* skinny. And she'd left her glasses on.

Then he saw her watching, taking stock of him as he was undressing. Not just the size of his various body parts. He saw her squinting in curiosity at his black hair and high, rounded cheekbones.

It was a look he knew by heart.

Afterward, she'd brought him a cigarette and they'd lain

smoking in bed. Then, finally, the question: "If you don't mind my asking, what *are* you?"

He'd toyed with her. "I'm a partner in a public relations firm. And an ex-journalist. Used to write for the *Chronicle*. Is that what you mean?"

"Not exactly."

"Well, I played some football. University of Kansas, offensive line. Perhaps you remember me from that."

"That's not what I'm really asking," she admitted. "It's more like…"

"Hey, I gotcha." He'd snickered sadly as he snuffed out his cigarette and drew a long leg out from beneath the covers. "I'm Nanticoke," he said as he stood up and reached for his pants. "It's a brand of Native American."

As he was lacing up his shoes, she seemed to be wrestling with another question. Her face was wrinkled up in puzzlement.

He understood. Black hair and rounded cheekbones were just about all the Indian features he could muster. In the right light, he could pass for white. Except for the flared nostrils, the extra fold of skin at the corners of his eyes. The nap in his hair, the slight cast of skin color—like the dust from red maple. In a dim light, he might appear black.

In truth, he was a hybrid. While he sometimes got angry when people stared at him, at other times he was fatalistic. That's what it meant to be Nanticoke—to be an enigma, the scion of a Delaware tribe that had mixed with blacks and whites for aeons. It was the black genes that had enabled the group to survive so many of the epidemics the full-blooded Indians had succumbed to. But to survive as what?

"Why, you're an American Mestee," the spectacled girl had blurted. "I'm taking a sociology course," she added.

"It's mess-tay," he said, as he buttoned his shirt and looked for his car keys. "That's how you pronounce it."

When he turned around, she was sitting bolt upright, the covers down to her waist. Her nipples were pink and excited.

She said, "I'm doing a paper, and it's fascinating. All these obscure groups in Appalachia, back in the hills, hidden away—the Brass Ankles, the Melungeons. What was it that demographer called them? I know: 'the tri-racial isolates.'"

He laughed darkly. "They can write that on my tombstone." He leaned down and kissed her on the forehead.

She reached up and trailed his hand across her breasts. "You know, I'm doing a paper," she murmured as he went out the door.

Now, as he stepped out of the shower on the morning after, Hawk thought of one other concept he might have taught the girl in glasses. It was something about "marginality."

The idea was that a person might pick up more in his surroundings if he failed to fit any single ethnic group. If he weren't locked into any one culture. If he didn't quite belong. That was the notion: that a guy on the fringes could see more. Maybe a backhanded blessing. A saving grace.

He took a long look at himself, as he toweled the mirror clean to shave. He nodded at the face that stared back. Yep, there was a marginal man, all right. But what did that mean? How much could he really see?

There was one thing he was sure of and it haunted him. Last night, he'd seen Denver in the dead of night, obliterated.

2

Wally Arneson called his mother every morning. Not to talk with her. In the state she was in, conversation was no option. But he checked in via video phone. They connected the call in the nursing home to a minicamera mounted on the wall of her room. It was written into his contract. Every morning, he could look in on his mother. Or on what was left of her. She lay sprawled on her side, scrawny as a scarecrow, her wispy hair splayed gray against the pillow.

It didn't take long to look for signs of neglect, for in fact there was very little he could see. Was the aspirator at the corner of her mouth? Was there a pool of drool there, or a yellow stain down lower on her bed sheet?

The whole process took less than a minute, though it might have been more had he ever taken time to reflect on his mother and the person she once had been. But Wally made the phone call as he brewed his morning coffee, and it took no time at all. The call was a way of connecting to an appalling situation. The crowded halls and wailing. The slop of pureed meals. And, oh my God, the smells. The nauseating, rancid stench of loose bowels and bladders. He'd visited the nursing home once. It had been more than he could stomach.

Wally had lived alone two years now, ever since Martha left. The video phone was his companion. In fact, every week or so, he'd dial up another number from a roster of phones just like it. There was a mounted camera in each room; a much younger woman; and, yes, a bed as well.

Wally had a habit of swiveling his head. He was a tall, gangling man with a large, bald head, a salt-and-pepper beard, and horn-rimmed glasses. There are tall men who seem born to their stature. They live up to their height and seem at ease when others look up to them. But that wasn't Wally.

When he was nine years old or so, he'd shot up like a dandelion as his parents watched in awe. They marveled at what a big man he'd be, when he grew up and filled out. Except he never did. But for a paunch that appeared on his abdomen in midlife, Wally stayed thin as a stick. The one part of him that had matured to full size was his head. Perhaps that was why he swiveled it whenever he met someone new or walked into a crowded room, scanning the environs like a lighthouse beacon.

As he arrived for work that Monday, the large room latticed with cubicles was abuzz with the Broncos' thrilling victory. But the susurration hushed as Wally stepped through the door. "Good morning, Mr. Arneson." "Howdy, Mr. Arneson." "Nice day, sir." There was a syncopated chorus of greetings every time Wally turned up at the department he headed at Telwest. The murmurs rose and fell all around the room as his head jerked erratically in every direction. It wasn't that his employees were intimidated by Wally Arneson. It was just that they were never sure in which direction he was looking.

"Good morning, sir," his secretary, Gloria, offered as he neared his office. Wally had a corner office that sat above most of the scattered high-rises in downtown Denver and overlooked the plains and foothills far out to the horizon. It was one of the few offices at Telwest that had a door, and the privacy was a comfort to Wally. He was one of those introverts-by-nature who awaken one day to find themselves in a job that threatens to involve them with people. He walked into his office, dusted off the sign on the door,

Manager: New Product Development. With an audible sigh, he shut it.

There was a knock on the door, and Gloria ventured in. She was a somewhat shapeless matron in her mid-fifties, with mouse-brown hair streaked with dishwater gray. Wally had hired her from a secret pool of secretarial candidates known to managers as the M&Ms. Married and menopausal, the most reliable support staff one could hope for.

Gloria stood at the entrance to Wally's office, quavering slightly and clutching a stack of pink slips with phone messages. She jutted her chin forward to clear her throat, then hesitated. Wally had waved her in, but now he was hunched over a credenza in the corner, peering at a device that looked to be a computer with a telephone touch pad. As he punched in a long string of numbers, the machine began to whirr and click. It made a wheezing sound, and a robotic voice uttered, "You are now connected." Then, slowly, a large, blue Telwest T began to take shape on the screen.

"Um, Mr. Arneson, you've had several calls."

Wally gave a start and looked up from the video phone. He shook his head and gave her a smug smile. "Some day, there'll be no need for those message slips, Gloria. You know, we're beta-testing a messaging system this week. I'll be able to log on and dial up the mug of every caller, along with whatever he has to say. I tell you... well, you know what I always say. We'll reinvent this company, this whole industry. I tell you, Gloria, we're not far off."

"That is so impressive, sir." Gloria gave a twitch and, beneath her sacklike blouse, her torso quivered like Jell-O. "Now, then, here are your messages. And I thought I would call your attention to this one on the top. It's from a Mr. Rowe, Granger Rowe. He said it was urgent."

Wally thought a moment. "Did he say who he was with?"

"Sir, I believe he's with Telwest. I've heard he's our new Vice President for Advanced Technology."

"A vice president…" Wally wrinkled his brow and cocked his head. "Might be my new boss—will you try to reach him for me?"

As she turned toward the door, Wally was back at his keypad. Sure enough, the beta test was underway. There was a list of messages on the video phone, and slowly the first began to squiggle into shape. Wally gazed deep into the screen and soon lost himself in the hum of the machine.

The phone buzzed. "It's the vice president on the line, sir."

Wally fumbled with his stack of messages. Finally he came up with the fellow's name. "Rowe, Granger Rowe." Should he call him "Sir?" "Mr. Rowe?" "Granger?"

How to address people was one of the questions he had about this management job. In fact, there were hordes of questions, and they all involved the baffling art of interacting with people. There had been a workshop on this subject just last week. They'd said to use the full name in correspondence and the first name in conversation. Or was it the full name in conversation on the first call?

He stared out his window as his head began to shift along the horizon, up and down the mountains. Finally, he took a deep breath and picked up the phone. He peered down at the message slip. And at last he croaked, "Hello?"

3

There were two ways to get downtown from Hawk's condominium in Cheesman Park. The most direct was to take the major business route, East Colfax Avenue. But Hawk didn't often go this way. No one from his neighborhood did. Colfax was the underside of the Mile High City—a flotsam of second-hand stores, porn shops, and fast food outlets that could make you suspect you'd left the rarified air of the Rocky Mountain West and been transported into the Bronx.

It was easy to skirt the ugliness and poverty of Colfax by taking 13th Avenue into town. You still arrived at the gold-domed capitol and the expanse of Civic Center Park but without the memory of the slum it had taken to get there.

Hawk exited the underground garage of his condo and started up 13th, but the road was packed in a half foot of melting snow. Reluctantly, he made his way two blocks north to Colfax. A main artery, it pulled rank on the other east-west streets and was always plowed, first thing in the morning.

The traffic was heavy on Colfax, and Hawk had time to look around as he drove into town. There was the Ogden Theater, empty these days except for the occasional grunge rock concert. He knew that this had been a popular theater ten years ago, with double features of art and foreign films. Colfax had been a haven for upscale restaurants: Mama Elena's for Mexican food, the Athenian for Greek. When the energy industry bit the dust in the eighties, there was a patina of culture that went down, too. A commercial jazz radio station, a vegetarian Italian restaurant...

He pulled up at a stoplight, four blocks from the state capitol, and noticed that the neighborhood took a step up. There was a new Office Depot on the south side of Colfax at Pearl Street. Must be the legislature's going into session, he was thinking. Look at that crowd in the parking lot. Legal pads on sale?

But just before the light changed, he looked over at the lot again. And he saw the fellows lined up all along Pearl Street. They weren't out there for office supplies. There was a pickup truck and people passing out provisions. Those men were standing there for food.

As he drove ahead on Colfax, Hawk felt a knot slowly form in his stomach. For a moment, he was a child again, in the early days of winter in Kansas. When his family had migrated from Rhode Island to the harsh land west of Wichita—to Kansas, where there was a Native American college. Back to that first winter, when there was nothing for breakfast and you huddled by the side of the road, for the school bus, the sharp wind whistling through your flimsy jacket and worn-out jeans.

He shuddered and snapped back into the present tense. Why did this happen? The visions. The mood swings. Denver in the daylight. Denver in the dark. Sometimes his life felt like a thin crust suspended over—? Something dark and ominous. And in this place... more days of sunshine per annum than San Diego.

"Morning, Teresa."

The trim brunette at the reception desk glanced up with a gleaming smile. How did Latin women stay so cheerful? Must be something in the salsa.

"*Buenos dias,* Hawk. *Cómo estás?*"

"Not bad, just thawing out. Took in the game last night and froze my tail feathers. Hey, is Todd in?"

"*Si, claro.*" She nodded in the direction of his business partner's office, and returned to the spreadsheet on her monitor. Teresa not only doubled as their bookkeeper, she trebled as the purchasing manager and generally ran the small company. Hawk had seen suppliers lose their accounts when they brushed her off and treated her like the help.

"He's in, but he ain't *ocupado*," Teresa added with a toss of her long black hair. There were times when he suspected their receptionist had designs on becoming personnel manager as well.

He set out for Todd's office, past shafts of sunlight that streamed through leaded windows, along the deep green carpet to the weathered brick walls on the far side of the reception room. The Hermitage was a nineteenth-century landmark in lower downtown, an area of dark warehouses that had come alive since the new baseball park opened. Rumor had it that the Hermitage had begun its life as a whorehouse, and that had only stoked its market value. In the glitz of Denver's new high-tech economy, there was a certain hunger for history—for any whiff of musty love and lust on the old frontier.

He rapped once and stepped into Todd's wood-paneled office. His partner was on the phone, peppering a conversation with animated gestures. Feet on his desk, he lay back so far in his Naugahyde chair he might have been getting a shave, or a blow job in the one-time boudoir. Todd raised his eyebrows and gestured toward the thirty-inch screen that filled the wall between two stuffed elk heads on the far side of his office.

There, on the TV, was John Elway redux—his touchdown pass, his postgame interview, then the talking heads of football analysts, chewing over everything he'd done and said, and what he might have meant when he said it.

Todd was wide-eyed as he hung up the phone and swiveled toward his partner. He ran a hand through his tousled hair and shook his head in wonder. At thirty-two, they were the same age and had been in business together for five years. But that's where the similarities ended. Sometimes it seemed they'd been living in different galaxies. Todd was a blond, blue-eyed Nordic who'd grown up in a small town in Wyoming. He was the kind of specimen a geneticist might call "clear-blooded."

"So, what'd you think, Hawk? How 'bout that Elway? Talk about a game! Makes you want to get out there and kick somebody's butt, right?"

He might have said the conventional "ass," but that wasn't Todd. "Butt" was as close to profanity as he got. When Todd was seven, his family had moved him along with his older brother and sister to Casper, Wyoming, far from the temptations of suburban Chicago. The transition was not entirely unsuccessful. Although his brother discovered a new supplier of drugs and his sister found a guy to get her pregnant, Todd got with the program and began pouring all his energies into hunting and fishing.

These days, his outdoor sports doubled as public relations. Todd seldom hefted a fishing rod or hoisted a rifle to his shoulder without a client close by.

Todd ran the television all day, albeit with the sound off. Film clips of hurricanes, ads for frozen dinners, head shots of newsreaders with frozen smiles parading past all day. While he ignored the TV most of the time, the procession of pictures was always there, a tableau to the rest of his life if not a subtext. Hawk wondered how many other broadcasting majors had a similar addiction.

"So, what's in the Daytimer?" Hawk asked as he flopped

down into a side chair. "Is this the week we get rich and retire?"

"Film crew scheduled at eleven o'clock," Todd responded. "Just a clip for the evening news. Bunch o' third graders out at the new animal shelter. You know, the one Telwest is bankrolling out there in Evergreen. The Broncos said they'd send over a couple of cheerleaders."

"In T-shirts, I trust. Be nice if the sun comes out and they can take off their jackets," Hawk muttered.

Tits, tots, and pets: it was a time-honored formula for television news coverage, and they both knew it well. Touch any one of those bases and your chances were enhanced on the nightly news. Todd had rounded the bases: cheerleaders, grade school kids, and animals in distress. For the pros who had worked on the other side of the street as journalists, public relations was not so much an art as a science. It was sinfully easy to manipulate the media.

"So, what about you?" Todd asked. "You're pumped, aren't you—'cause the Broncos won, and all? I mean, you did go to the game...didn't you? Geez, sometimes I can't believe you even played, much less..."

"I've been trying to contain my excitement," Hawk responded, dryly. "But, sure, I could use a good goose the way the day's shaping up. Nothing but a stack of these fucking sponsorships to shuffle through. The damned things have been piling up on my desk. Same cast of characters, all the do-gooders in town lined up at the philanthropic trough. Sometimes I think if it weren't for Telwest, these guys would have to make an honest living."

"I know, I know," Todd said. "But if it weren't for Telwest, you and I might be..." He left the sentence hanging.

Hawk felt a twinge as he completed it. "In the same bread line. Or, at least I would." In his mind's eye, he caught a glimpse of the line-up outside Office Depot.

"You know, podner," Todd said, "it wouldn't hurt if you'd think about turning up some new business."

"Oh, come on, do we have to go through this again?" Hawk objected.

"Look, you don't have to call folks up on the phone or anything," Todd went on. "But when you go to the gym, say, strike up a conversation in the juice bar after you work out. Don't just sit there like you do and stare off into space."

"Okay, so what do you want me to do? Carry a sign with a commercial? Maybe a sandwich board, although it could be a little tough on the treadmill." Hawk had pulled himself to his feet and was walking toward the door.

"Hawk, I'm serious. Buy somebody a carrot drink. Pass out your card. Tell lies about your football days. Let 'em know we're still in circulation."

This was a conversation they had every two or three weeks, and it felt like a religious rite that no one continued to believe in. Hawk couldn't sell toilet paper in a toilet. He wasn't cut out for business development, and he knew it. So might Todd, if he'd ever turn off the TV long enough for thirty seconds of reflection.

"Look, Todd. We've been through this before." Hawk had opened the door but he shut it again. He walked back to Todd's desk and looked down at him. "You and I are a typical partnership. You are the guy who rustles up clients. And I am the guy who stays in and does the work. Sometimes it's not exciting work, but I stay here and I do it. Speaking of which, it's already 10:30, and I need to get back to my desk." He headed for the door.

"So, go out and get some new work, Hawk. Bring in some business. You know that's all I'm saying," Todd hollered after him.

Hawk waved him off as he walked away. Their tiff today had been especially heated, and he wondered why. Did Todd know something he didn't?

4

Hawk stared at the stack of proposals that teetered at the far edge of his desk. There were bound and printed folders of every size and shape in a panoply of eye-catching colors. This was not his favorite part of his job, but there it was and he did it. Every month, he sifted through a pile of these funding requests addressed to Telwest from the altruists of Denver. There were walkathons to combat dreadful diseases, halfway houses for glue-sniffing addicts, resume workshops for geologists who—ten years after the collapse of the oil and gas industry—still had not found employment.

Hawk would faithfully peruse their plans to save the planet, pick out maybe half a dozen proposals, then summon a committee from the new product development department of Telwest. They'd horse around for a couple of hours, swilling soft drinks and scarfing down peanuts on company time. Then they'd get around to rank-ordering the proposals. They'd take a second look at their budget and fund one maybe every three months.

Wally Arneson, Hawk's one client, was a manager in new product development, and he loved these committee meetings. Hawk was never sure why. Was it the idea of doing good works? Or that he didn't have much of a social life outside his job? Perhaps it was just a chance to hobnob with his employees. The one incontrovertible fact was that Hawk's agency was paid a goodly sum for the grunt work of wading through the proposals so that Wally now and then could fund one.

With a Monday morning groan, Hawk pulled the first proposal off the stack—lavender with purple ink. He winced. Bad choice. Purple was the color of the Kansas State Wildcats, sworn rival of KU. How many times had he faced off against some behemoth clad in purple, pawing and snorting on the defensive line. Purple! As he riffled the pages of the garish grant proposal, his mind went tumbling back to college days. He thought of Todd when he'd first known him, and how things had evolved. And of how the hell he'd landed in this partnership.

They had met at the University of Kansas, one of the best journalism schools in the country. While their diplomas listed the same major, their training was as different as Colorado and Kansas—the mountains and the plains. Todd was a broadcasting major, Hawk in traditional, print journalism. In broadcasting, you studied the way things looked and sounded—how to package information in short bursts of video clips and sound bites. The news became a succession of peak moments, stark against the sky.

Print journalism was a different profession, or so Hawk had been led to believe. There, you worked for days, maybe weeks, drudging through data, digging out the roots of a story. The process could be as monotonous as the plains, but when you finished, you generally had something to say.

He'd met Todd their senior year, when both happened to be assigned a project on tornadoes. Had it not been for that single assignment, it was likely their paths would not have crossed. Todd was into Greek Street, president of his fraternity. With a thatch of flaxen hair and an engaging smile, he never lacked companionship.

Hawk had lived in a gritty world of analgesic balm, training tables, and practice fields—until he quit football. From then on, it was hard to tell where he might be found, except for occasional excursions into the Native

American Cultural Center or the Black Student Union, neither of which quite fit him. For the most part, he kept to himself.

Hawk had been sent out to interview experts on the subject of tornadoes, meteorologists who kept up with changes in the climate of eastern Kansas and the violent storms that swept through the region each spring.

Todd was told to chase a tornado—not so much to photograph the storm as to capture the sensations surrounding it. It was your basic, human interest story. He came upon one young woman, a thin, wan blond, not long after her trailer had been hit. She was bruised and dazed, her blouse torn down to a bra strap, lying waist deep in the cheap wood paneling and flimsy struts which, moments before, had been her home.

Todd had pulled her from the wreckage, flashed a comforting smile, and located her cat. By the time he finally pulled out his mike, her story flowed onto the video tape and then over the evening news in Kansas City.

Hawk, meanwhile, had dug out the subtext, the reasons tornadoes were becoming more frequent and violent, the need for higher standards in the manufacture of mobile homes. When the two received As at the end of the term, it was an anticlimax. For the project had got them their first jobs, and launched what appeared to be can't-miss careers in journalism.

"So much for history," Hawk muttered as he thought about his one job on a newspaper—and how he'd loved it. It was the one place he'd felt at home, for a while. He remembered his fellow reporters—that bunch of misfit, aging hippies in baggy sweaters and threadbare jeans. And Art Branscomb, the ex-psychiatrist-turned-columnist who polluted the whole department with a fog of alcohol every time he exhaled. He smiled as he thought of Art, his friend.

But he remembered how the job had ended, and that catapulted him back into the present tense. He took one more look at the purple proposal, tossed it on the floor, and started to reach for the next one.

He thought of something. Maybe there was a way to stay on task and get organized. Hawk flicked on his computer and called up a file with a template of criteria. One of the programmers on the committee had come up with it last month. He looked over the list of questions.

- Will the project appeal to our customers?
- Does it have a logical link with our company?
- What kind of media coverage does the project offer? (Think TV spots to logos on T-shirts.)
- What are the chances of it being successful? (No need for negative publicity.)
- Are important customers involved? (Think society-page photo-ops.)

There were maybe a dozen items like that, and he printed off a copy of the template. He spent a few minutes modifying the form, adding a column for scoring each item and a space for making comments in the margins. He liked this part of public relations: the systematic, almost scientific side of the field. He experimented by ranking a few on a scale of one to five.

Still, he couldn't get past that incident with Todd. What if he did have to rustle up clients, to find the work as well as do it? What if Telwest... The questions pressed in, encircling him.

There was a tap on the door and Teresa was there. "Ah, so deep in thought, *amigo*. Sometimes, I wonder, when you are with us, but you stare away in space... I wonder where you go. Ah, well, it is as they say: *En cada cabeza es un mundo*—'There is a world in every head.'"

Hawk looked up with a grin. "Is that what they say? By the way, I'm working on a collection of all your proverbs—400 so far, and counting."

She nodded solemnly as she handed him a slip of paper. "And where is your head, *amigo*? Perhaps this is a *mensaje* from over there."

Hawk looked at the message as she turned and left. "Call Lance Ralston: URGENT." For an instant, his eyes grew bright and his spirits lifted.

Ralston was an old teammate who had hooked up with the Broncos as a media relations specialist. It was the kind of job that many a fan would pay any price to have, especially an ex-jock. To be back on the gridiron, even if only on the sidelines. But he didn't know that much about what Lance did.

He picked up the phone. It was an odd number. Probably one of those cellular phones that people carried around with them. Hawk had read about this trend the other day. The article said that nowadays ten percent of Americans had one of these gizmos. Some predicted the percentage would double, maybe triple, in ten years.

Hawk frowned as the phone rang. Imagine keeping a telephone in your car, in your pocket. Turning itself on and ringing at odd times. *En cada cabeza es un mundo.* What would happen to your life inside your head?

Finally, Lance picked up the phone. There was screaming in the background, the hiss of water streaming from a shower, a loud joke and raucous laughter. Hawk felt a wave of nostalgia.

"Hello?" said Lance, as someone let a fart.

"It's Hawk."

"Oh, my God. Thanks for calling. Listen, I know this is short notice, but can you come down here in an hour? What is it now, about eleven o'clock? No, a half-hour; 11:30, the press is coming. At the practice facility—you know, Dove

Valley. Jesus, Hawk, I hate to ask you. I know you're busy. Shit. Hold on a minute..."

The noise mounted: a cacophony of cheers and boos, to the echoes of whap, whap, whap. Hawk recognized the tumult of a towel fight. Then he heard a door slam and all was quiet.

"Hawk, you still there? I'm back in my office. Look, we've got the press coming—open locker room—and I don't know what to do about this wide receiver. Benjie Green. Did you see him on TV? First touchdown pass he's caught all season, so nobody's interviewed him. But, holy Jesus, wait until they do. This guy is... well, you'll see."

Lance apologized again, and promised to buy Hawk a good lunch. Hawk shrugged as he hung up the phone. The morning was shot. This was no way to get through the proposals. But he'd promised Lance he'd be there.

The Broncos' practice facility was on a dusty, treeless road at the south end of a flotilla of suburban office buildings known as the Denver Technological Center. The football complex consisted of a two-story building that housed the team offices, locker room, and training facilities; an outdoor football field with no stands; and a second field for practices in foul weather.

The operation looked relentlessly suburban, and Hawk thought that was by design. Aside from the goal posts that jutted up behind the Broncos' building and the enormous, white vinyl bubble that loomed over the indoor practice field, the office complex seemed like an insurance firm or a cable TV company. One more bland entity in the corporate world.

To be sure, there were certain practical advantages to housing the team in the suburbs south of Denver. The complex in Dove Valley was close to where most of the players lived, in big split-levels on sprawling tracts of what not long ago had been ranch land. So, it was a short commute in to the training facility. And it was a good half-hour from the major bars and other blandishments of the city itself.

But Hawk knew the real reason for locating in a corporate office park. It was to project a big-league image for the team. For Denver was still, in many respects, a minor league sports town. To be sure, there was a franchise in every one of the major league sports: baseball, basketball, football, and hockey. But the baseball and hockey teams were new in the nineties. And, although the Broncos had more than thirty years of history under their belts, they still often seemed like interlopers, compared to the storied NFL franchises in places like Chicago and Philadelphia and New York.

Part of it was the way the team had struggled to survive in the early days. Back in the sixties, someone had sold the Broncos a stock of uniforms with striped socks: vertical stripes that made the players look like mannequins. A roar went in the stands wherever the Broncos appeared. They were laughing socks.

Finally, the Broncos had had enough. At a preseason game on a summer night in 1964, they built a bonfire at the south end of the stadium. They carted in the whole pile of striped socks, saving one pair that would land in a museum, and burned the lot at half time. The socks, of course, had served their purpose. They'd brought press coverage to the Broncos and the fledgling American Football League, a public relations bonanza.

Today, the Broncos were a perennial Super Bowl contender with a quarterback headed for the Hall of Fame. But they still played their home games in a creaking old stadium, the last vestige of their early days. Originally a minor league baseball park, Mile High Stadium had been expanded on and on—like a giant Erector set—into a huge, metallic structure that rattled in the cold winds of the late season and shook to the foundations when fans pounded their feet on the aluminum floorboards.

Sure, a new stadium was on the drawing board. But every game at Mile High evoked a day, not many decades ago, when pro football was still something of an oddity and the Broncos were an outfit dressed in striped socks, a franchise somewhat stranger than the rest.

Hawk walked into a lobby with a high, vaulted ceiling and checked in at the reception desk. He was handed a press credential—a large, laminated tag with a clasp that attached to his belt loop. The receptionist called for Lance on the intercom, and in a minute his old teammate appeared. He was a solid, crew-cut fellow who looked every inch the former college fullback. Hawk suspected he worked out with the team.

Lance flashed a smile of relief when he saw his old offensive lineman, but his brow was furrowed all the same. He stood at the door to the locker room and waved for Hawk to follow. The place was carpeted and more commodious than any locker room Hawk had seen. But the air was redolent of sweat-soaked jockstraps and the wintergreen aroma of pain-relieving ointments.

At the first whiff of the locker room, Hawk felt some memories surface. He understood why Lance would have taken this job.

"I don't know how this is going to go," Lance told him, "but you know it's part of my job to baby-sit these guys. I think they call it 'media relations.' I'd like you to see how this Benjie relates to the reporters, and if we maybe need to coach him some."

Lance led Hawk to a spot behind a pillar in the center of the room, a half dozen feet from Benjie's locker. He watched as the clock showed 11:30 and the press poured in like an avalanche. There were grungy-looking newspaper reporters in sweatshirts, with notepads and mini-tape recorders; TV journalists, dressed to the nines, with camera crews. Several of the reporters were women.

The journalists were old hands in the locker room, and they knew where to look for every player. A dozen of them massed around the locker of John Elway, a demigod whose every sneeze would be reported.

At the other end of the room, a few clusters of Bronco linemen sat in uncomfortable isolation. Sometimes they'd facetiously pretend to interview one another. As with every football team, the defensive line never drew much attention, and the offensive linemen even less. This year, for some reason, their coach had forbidden them to speak to reporters. It was like fasting in a famine, Hawk thought. As though anyone wanted to hear what they had to say.

In the middle of the room, the ends held sway and Hawk watched Benjie Green in front of his locker. He stood there, bouncing up and down on his heels, as he peered down at the mob surrounding Elway. Benjie was wearing nothing but a towel around his waist.

Hawk wondered if Green was studying Elway. The tall quarterback had an infectious, buck-toothed grin, and he greeted each of the reporters personably. When one of the young radio reporters asked him for an interview, Elway said he had to decline; he was under contract to a rival radio station. Then he tried to soothe the kid: "Hey, man—you know, I always listen to your station."

If the Broncos' locker room resembled an overgrown recreation room in a suburban subdivision, why, Elway seemed just the sort of guy you'd be pleased to have as a neighbor, to hobnob with over the back fence.

Before long, the first few reporters drifted down Green's way, and Hawk drew back behind his pillar to see how the young receiver handled himself. In an instant, he found out that the kid was in way over his head.

"So, how'd it feel to snare that pass from Elway?" asked a TV reporter, his mike in Benjie's face, the cameras rolling. "Tell us about it."

Green stared at the newsman, incredulous. Then he snapped, "Shit, man, you was at the game. You seen it. I done deeked that motha-fucka at the twenty—left him in the snow bank. Just laid him on his ass."

The reporter shuddered. Well, at least this wasn't live; there was time for editing.

"But, tell us, Benjie. What were you thinking when you caught that pass?"

The receiver looked dumbfounded. "Thinking? Hey, man, you can't be thinkin' when you deekin', puttin' some dude on his ass."

The TV newsman shook his head and moved aside, as a young blonde from the *Denver Post* stepped up to Benjie, notebook in hand. She offered Green a wide-eyed smile, and he gave her a smirk in return.

"Well, Benjie..." she started, then froze. There was a flurry of fuzzy white as the receiver tugged at the terry cloth on his waist. Benjie Green stood grinning, naked as a doorknob, his towel splayed out on the floor.

They had beers and beef brisket sandwiches down the road from the Broncos' at the County Line Barbecue. It was a warm, autumn day and they sat out back. As he mopped the sauce from his mouth with a clutch of napkins, Hawk tried to think of what to say. For a long time, he stared off into the aspen trees that lined the patio. Lance seemed a bit downcast, but now and then he looked up at Hawk expectantly.

Finally, he thought of how to break the news. "Do you remember what coach used to say about how athletes develop? 'To be coachable means you're able to receive new information.' Does that ring any bells?"

Lance nodded.

"Well, I'll give it to you without the window dressing. I don't think our Benjie Green is at what you'd call 'a teachable moment.' You could try to tell him something, or I could, and it'd be time wasted. This guy's enthralled with who he is right now. We can't teach him anything about how to be interviewed."

Lance's face fell. "So, what do I do? You know how it is: people want to know how it feels to be a jock. 'What were you thinking when you caught that pass? What were you feeling? How are you feeling now?' And it's even worse ever since that media outfit bought the Nuggets: The Summit Group. It's not like we're playing football anymore. We're in show biz. Man, this is song and dance in jockstraps."

Hawk nodded. "But when it comes to Benjie, we have to consider how we cast him. The main thing is, we keep him off camera in the locker room. Tell the coaches to get him the hell out of there when the media comes around."

"And then?"

"Let's create a new venue," Hawk said. "Look, I have a charitable event coming up with Telwest. I don't know which one they'll fund yet, but whatever it is, it'll make the evening news. Suppose we put Benjie front and center. Comforting an injured eagle, calling on kids in the hospital."

"And that'll get me off the hook?" asked Lance.

Hawk nodded again. "It'll get him on camera, silent film. That's one thing we'll make sure of—whatever he does, he won't have to say a damn thing while he's doing it."

As he drove back up the freeway to Lower Downtown, Hawk felt almost euphoric. What a great feeling, to be back in the world of sports where rhetoric took a back seat to performance. After all, if Benjie started dropping those passes, there'd be no one there to notice if he let go of his towel. He gave his steering wheel a slap. That was the real world, all right.

Then he cringed from an unwelcome memory.

Hawk could still see the leering grin of that monstrous nose guard, the last game of his junior year. The guy was a behemoth, and he seemed menacing as hell as he pawed the ground across the line, snorting up mucous and spewing it on the wet grass. But he looked a little thick around the midriff. Might be slow on his feet.

Hawk remembered his astonishment as the ball was snapped. The nose guard took off like a wounded water buffalo, careening around him and slamming the KU halfback to the turf. It was painful to miss your blocking assignment, but on somebody that size who had no right to be that fast...

Until that day, Hawk had pretty much defined himself as a football player and had reveled in his press clippings: "Can't miss NFL draft pick. Projected for the first or second round..." Yet, this guy had left him in the dust.

But that wasn't the worst of it. There was the burst of anger that had flared up into rage and engulfed him like a brush fire. He'd leg-whipped the nose guard on the following play, and he remembered the sick sense of satisfaction as he watched them carry the poor bastard off on a golf cart. The other KSU linemen looked on, glowering. "Watch your ass, Tonto!"

For the first and last time, Hawk had had second thoughts about his future in the game. He'd walked off the field and hung up his cleats. It was the start of a long journey to find another path in life, but had he found it? He thought of Art Branscomb, the one-time psychiatrist. If he could catch him in a moment of sobriety, his friend might have a theory about that.

He arrived back at the office about three o'clock, hoping to complete the work he'd begun on the proposals. Hoping he'd missed Todd, as well. His partner had said something about taking off for a couple of days of pheasant hunting in Nebraska, and Hawk thought they could use the time apart. In a partnership of two, there weren't a lot of places for either of them to hide.

But Todd was still there, and as Hawk sat down at his desk and sorted through a stack of mail, he stuck his head in. This time he was grinning broadly.

"So, you took my advice, Big Chief. Teresa said you were out at the Broncos'. Business development—all right! I knew you had it in you."

Hawk stared at him, perplexed. "I was just down seeing Lance."

"Sure, sure, I know," Todd went on. "I've heard his name before—PR guy, right? Well, that's the name of the game. Cultivate those corporate clients. Build up our billable hours. So, what's he paying us?"

Hawk looked down a moment and then he leaned back in his chair. "He bought my lunch. It's not like he's a client."

Todd's grin twisted a little. Hawk could feel his own gut tighten and the bile rise in his throat.

"He bought your lunch." Todd reflected. "Hawk, when it comes to public relations, you're probably the best technician in town. And the Broncos are loaded. That owner of theirs? He's a multimillionaire. But, no, he's not a client."

"He's a friend. The guy had a problem with the media and one of his players, and I helped him out a little. I'd do the same thing again. Do you know who Lance is? He was my fullback, and I was his lineman. Back in Kansas. I blocked for him. But I don't suppose you could understand that."

Todd had turned his back and started out the door. As he came to the hall, he paused as if to say something more. Then he threw up his hands and kept walking.

5

Wally turned his head and listened intently as he watched his office door. The squeaking sound outside seemed to have caught his attention. For a long time, he had been deep in thought, lost in the view from his office on the 30th floor, watching the weather take shape. He'd been staring out over the skyline, past the green foothills splashed with aspen turning gold, out toward the leaden mountains on the far horizon. The caps of white snow glistened in the morning sun, and they were larger than the day before. Far off, over the crested peaks, a cloud bank was building into a snowstorm.

Wally wondered how much of the storm would funnel through to Denver. He loved to match wits with the weather-guessers on the evening news, and sometimes he placed bets with the programmers.

Today it seemed he could almost feel the wind, as he listened to his teeth chattering. He was chilled by what he'd just heard on the phone. But there it was, the squeak again. As he turned toward the door, he gave a weak smile. Now he recognized the sound. It was Gladys, the Office Mom, with her bright red Radio Flyer wagon. He shuffled through his desk drawer where he kept his little can of 3-in-One oil.

Hiring an Office Mom had been Wally's idea. He'd read about it in one of the half dozen business magazines he pored over each month. "Management by magazine article"—that was how his critics on the staff sometimes mocked him. But they never took issue with Gladys.

The Office Mom came by the wood-paneled employee lounge that occupied the center of Wally's video phone department twice a day with snacks and sodas. Sometimes she planned birthday parties for the programmers, as well. There were a dozen of them on his staff, and each one had a private office with a full-length window to gaze out over the mountains or the plains—a break from constantly pounding on a keyboard and staring at a screen.

The challenge was to get them to take breaks in the company of one another. Programmers were a solitary lot, often locked in their heads, and you had to keep tabs on them constantly. That's what Wally had found. A programmer might get off on a string of code that ran on and on through a symphony of brilliant logarithms. He might forget to eat, neglect to bathe, fall asleep on the floor of his office only to come up with a program that had absolutely nothing to do with the project at hand. A buzzer that went off when the sun went down. Or a clock at the corner of a video screen with a face that changed colors.

Enter the Office Mom, luring the reclusive nerds to the wood-paneled lounge, where they might scratch and grunt in the company of one another. Gladys knocked once and swung the door open without waiting for a reply.

"Hello, Wally." She greeted her boss with a soft smile that faded a little as she picked up on his mood. He presented the oilcan.

"Aw, you've got just what I need for my squeaky place. You always do...don't you, Wally." Gladys laid a hand on the corner of his desk, just above his knee. She was a firm-bodied woman of fifty with frosted hair and a size forty bra with a cup size that the programmers pegged at quad D. As Gladys leaned over to pick up the can, Wally drew a deep breath that whistled through his nostrils.

"Say, those do smell good," he murmured, then shot a glance at the wagon. "The cinnamon rolls."

Tuesday morning meant the weekly staff meeting. There would be the usual agenda: scheduling, equipment upgrades, progress reports. And for the programmer who'd written the most lines of usable code, there'd be an extra cinnamon roll. Wally sighed as he slowly got to his feet. He smiled sadly at Gladys. The Office Mom, the programmers. How much they felt like family.

He tried not to think about Granger Rowe.

6

Hawk finished his final review of the funding proposals. Assigning them numbers against the template he'd designed, he set them in rank order for the third time. It was more work than he'd needed to do, but the process was precise and predictable. For a while, it filled his mind and crowded out a problem, name of Todd.

What was up with his partner lately? Todd was due back from his hunting trip this afternoon. Would he still be so agitated?

There was a knock on the door and Teresa swept in with the morning mail, along with her sparkling smile.

"Ah, *muy ocupado, jefe grande!*" she said. "I'm sorry to disturb you."

"Teresa, you are always a welcome interruption." Hawk looked up with a grin. "Even though I know you just called me 'Big Chief.'"

She said, "I don't mean to be nosey, but here's this envelope from Haskell All Nations University. Isn't that where you started out in college?"

"That's right, before I got my scholarship and transferred to KU." Hawk glanced at the envelope with a frown. "I'll lay you odds this is about money."

He stuck the envelope from Haskell at the bottom of his mail. Finally, he opened it reluctantly. Christ, he'd sent them a check three months ago.

But the mailing was a different kind of solicitation. It seemed his *alma mater* was beefing up its course offerings in business. They cited some interesting trends in Native American business, viz. gambling casinos. It seemed that, although the casinos were garnering $10 billion a year for North American tribes, three quarters of the jobs were going to non-Indians.

Another chapter in the saga of exploitation. Hawk had tired of ain't-it-awful statistics, and he started to throw the flyer away. But something caught his eye: a new internship program. It seemed employers could sign up to hire recent graduates of the business program for a three-month assignment. Half the salary would be covered by a grant from the federal government. Sort of a three-month, on-the-job interview.

Not a bad idea. Suppose he could get a graduating business major. What's more, he could charge the employer's half of the paycheck to his client. As he read on, he found they had specific student in mind. It was a marketing major, a young woman twenty-four years old.

He took a moment to fill out the form and took it to Teresa.

"You know, I doubt Telwest would be up for hiring an intern from a school they've probably never heard of. But what the hell. Let's fax this over to Wally and give it a shot."

It was eleven o'clock—almost lunchtime, but not quite. He could hang around the office, waiting for Todd. But his mind flashed back to the Broncos in the locker room, how they carried their weight, buffed to the nines. He could be, too, if he'd work on his midriff. Hawk grabbed his gym bag and headed out the door. There was just time to get in a workout before lunch.

Friendly's Abs Lab was a three-block walk down Blake Street: a narrow, brick-paved road where dark warehouses had begun sprouting patios with ficus trees and umbrellas splashed with ads for Mexican beers.

The gym was a former tannery. Its two-story front wall had been carved up and fitted with an enormous picture window. Both floors were filled wall to wall with stationary running tracks, the kind where you adjust your speed to match your stamina on a given day. Today, as lunch hour gave way to early afternoon, the tracks were bouncing with glistening bodies clad in everything from black leotards to dirty, gray sweat suits, depending on the age, gender, and shapeliness of the wearer and each one's agenda for the day.

In Denver's come-and-get-it culture, Friendly's was a great place to see and be seen. Hawk ogled the joggers as he stepped inside. Flushed and puffing, they looked alert as feral cats—glancing up and down the street for someone they might know. To be seen in Friendly's, not just in the doorway with a gym bag, but pounding it out up there on the treadmill, was to firm up one's image as a denizen of the Rocky Mountain West. It had the same impact as an eight-cylinder SUV in the drive.

There was a line to get in the gym this day—often the case when the Broncos won—and Hawk moved in behind a couple of young women in orange jogging suits trimmed in blue. One of them was red-faced and panting, not from exertion but from the story she'd brought to tell.

"So I ask her, 'Where are you and Josh off to for the holidays?' You know, it's still early but most people have made some plans. And she goes, 'You mean you haven't heard?' She says, 'You know, it wasn't just Josh.'"

"I go, 'Whadda ya mean: have I heard what?'" The jogger leaned into her listener who stood transfixed, pony tail bobbing, undulating in place.

"And she goes, 'The Strategic Planning Department. I mean, it wasn't just Josh.'"

"I'm like, 'Josh? What's up with Josh?'"

"And then she unloads. It's all of them. Everybody in

that department got their notice last week. They're shutting down the whole department. I mean, how sad is that!"

Hawk changed into his gym clothes and slowly mounted the stairs toward the treadmasters on the second floor. He pondered what he'd heard, thinking of his vision of the Telwest sign, Sunday night. But just then, he caught sight of a man in a sweat-stained shirt stepping off a treadmill. The fellow flashed a grin as he waved toward Hawk. "She's all yours," he hollered. Hawk gave a nod as he climbed aboard and dialed into the controls.

As the track began to pick up speed, he considered that exchange—the guy's cheerful greeting and his own abrupt response. He knew he could do better as he listened to Todd, somewhere back in his head. "Go out there and make contacts. Make contacts, make contacts: the rhythm of his running shoes slapping the track.

There was a flash of blue at the corner of his eye as a jogger stepped off the next treadmill and another climbed on. Hawk glanced at the new runner, a short, pudgy guy with a thatch of blond hair that splayed out like a cornstalk. Then he noticed the fellow's bright blue T-shirt with a big-beaked bird: the Kansas Jayhawk. Hawk lowered his head to his chest. Oh, God, a fellow alum.

The corn-fed jogger was adjusting his speed, incline, and time dials when he happened to glance Hawk's way. There was a pause before he looked again.

"Say, aren't you? Oh, gimme a minute ... Hawk! Hawk Kidree! How ya doin', Big Chief?"

At first, Hawk regarded the runner impassively, till he began to feel something inside himself go stale and sour. He reached for the control panel on his treadmill, lowered the speed for thirty seconds, and pushed Stop. Slowly, he stepped in front of the next treadmill, facing the jogger.

"Do I know you?" he asked with a faint smile.

The new runner was wide-eyed, grinning broadly. His

track was moving slowly, still at warm up speed. "Well, not exactly, but I remember you. Oklahoma State? Your junior year? Hey, I was a junior, too, and I'll never forget..."

Hawk stared at the fellow, felt his abdomen tighten. This was the time to take stock of his emotions, to get under control. But he couldn't stand these fucking, feckless fans. Saturday sycophants who wouldn't give you the skin off a turnip any other day—who'd look right by you if you hadn't played ball.

The bile was rising in his throat now as he felt for the control panel on the jogger's treadmill, still holding his gaze and listening intently as the fellow nattered on. Slowly, he inched his thumb toward the speed dial.

"And then that Iowa State game, that was another..." Hawk kept pressing the dial. The fat fan's face was turning from pink to lobster as he tried to dredge up memories of his college days. The speed was increasing. "But, why'd you...give it up, Chief...so, so fast and just when..."

He was running: quick steps, full stride. Until, with a sonorous belch, the fat fan stumbled from the treadmill and fell to all fours. For a moment, he swayed a little. With a moan, he spewed out his lunch all over the floor.

Hawk cringed as he turned away. He took a quick shower and got himself dressed. As he made his way upstairs from the locker room, he glanced over at the snack bar, the meeting and greeting. The shock of what he'd just done made him quiver.

"Strike up a conversation in the juice bar. Buy somebody a carrot drink. Pass out your card. Tell lies about your football days. Let 'em know we're alive. If it wasn't for Telwest..."

He could hear Todd all the way from Nebraska.

7

"Catastrophizing!" The strange word rattled around the rough edges of Art Branscomb's whiskey voice and it carried a kind of comfort. Hawk had called his friend midafternoon. He always tried to catch him between the times he filed his column and fled for the bar, and today he was lucky.

"You're just making a catastrophe out of coincidence," the crusty ex-psychiatrist went on. "So you had a vision—not the first, as I recall. And you take pride in your premonitions. You see more than most folks. It's a race thing, am I right? You're Nanticoke."

"Art, it's not just what I saw that night."

"All right, you told me what you heard that gal say down at the health club. Now, if you catch me in a dark mood—say, an hour and a half from now when I've had a few shots down at the Press Club—I might buy your premise. There's a lot to be wary of when people start losing their jobs. I saw it all around here when the oil and gas business went down. Every shrink in town did."

"Well, that's what I mean," Hawk interjected. "I told you about the line-up for food outside the Office Depot, right over here on Pearl Street."

"Okay, so you saw that, too. But only 'cause you're looking for it. Hawk, our brains are like a virgin forest. We make our own paths through the wilderness in there. And right now, you're going in a circle, round and round. Now, you call me when something bad happens to *you*. Then you can tell me all about your visions."

The conversation settled him. The man had a knack for answering only the question you asked, and never asking more of you. That was good, for, at the moment, there were some things he'd done that he'd rather leave back in the wilderness. As he hung up the phone, he put his feet up on the desk and closed his eyes. He sank back in his chair.

There was a forest, thick with fir trees, where a football game was being played. The floor of the forest was carpeted with ferns, and Hawk felt their soft fronds as he rolled from his stomach to his back. He'd been beaten on the play; he knew that. But there was comfort in this field—a cushion and a balm.

Some of the trees were junipers, gangly and tall as cranes, with dark pointed limbs like witch hats and clumps of pale green berries. There was a soft breeze through the trees, and they were swaying in a herky-jerk, spasmodic sort of dance. Now and then, high up on a tree trunk, a face vaguely took shape as the branches parted.

Hawk thought he saw a familiar figure at one point, the craggy features of his old line coach in college. But the coach began to fade away and Okee, the great dark spirit of the Nanticokes, appeared. The god seemed to give a leering grin, then grimaced as he evanesced in the dark mass of the forest. Hawk shivered as he recognized Okee, the evil one. Insidious, above him, inside him.

Now he found himself gazing at a clump of lacy ferns ruffling along the sidelines. Soon they took shape, as well. Not with faces, but bodies: the limbs and torsos of all sorts of women he had known, beautiful breasts and buttocks. The ferns seemed to be sighing softly as they hovered above a large, oblong object that might have been a leg in knee pads. The leg was twisted at an odd angle, as though wrenched from its socket.

Was it his? Or the Kansas State lineman he'd leg-whipped

that day. He felt no pain, just watching the leg. He thought of the women and felt nothing.

It was about then he heard the voice, and saw the bird poking its head through the ferns. It was a jayhawk—clad in orange, with a big yellow beak and a thatch of hair the color of corn silk. The bird was bobbing up and down. It was clearly agitated, upset over something.

"Look at you," the jayhawk cawed. "Just look at you!"

Hawk swiveled in his desk chair and slowly cracked an eye. Rays of light from the late afternoon filtered through the fronds of a hanging fern and splayed against the red brick walls of his office. The figure came into focus.

Todd was leaning across the desk, shaking his head, his blond hair bobbing. He was in orange overalls. His face was cracked in a smile, but it was a crooked grin that Hawk knew well, the kind that could twist into a grimace.

"So, look at you. I take off for a couple of days of pheasant hunting, bent out of shape in a duck blind, and—three o'clock in the afternoon—look where I find you."

"Hullo, Todd." Hawk blinked at the outlandish overalls. "Did you bag anything?" And he thought: "or does it matter?" He imagined it had to have been a damn sight more exciting than mucking through these funding proposals. He cleared a path within a foot-high stack of laminated, multicolored binders and motioned for his partner to sit down.

"Can't stay," Todd sputtered, "Gotta line of voice messages and emails as long as your arm. But I had to stop by—give you a heads-up, *amigo*."

Todd sat still long enough to debrief the hunting trip. It had been a typical excursion up Interstate 25 to I-80. Over to Sidney, then on into the sand hills of Nebraska. Hawk knew the routine Todd followed. There'd be steaks in a road house, neon lit in red and blue and amber and awash in Coors Light. Overnight in a farm house at the edge of the pine ridge that etched a spine down through western

Nebraska. Then up before dawn to do nothing all day but wait, hunkered down in the blinds, for the pheasants.

There was a way to hunt and bring home some game. With an ear cocked for a bird call or the flutter of wings, you spoke only in hushed tones. There was a discipline. But not with clients. As the day wore on to the pop and fizz of beer tabs, the talk would grow louder. To hunt was to network. That was Todd's philosophy. It was nothing like his boyhood in Wyoming. His hunting parties were a great place to hang out if you were a pheasant into longevity.

"So, it was two guys from Telwest," Todd was saying. "Dan Russell. You've met him, V. P. of Marketing. And of course the CIO, Vern Warner." Todd settled back into his seat with a smug smile. As he clasped his hands behind his head, two dark ovals appeared in his armpits. Hawk got up and cracked a window. In addition to the figure he cut in his overalls, Todd smelled the part of a hunter.

But he understood the value of the junket his partner had put together. He'd met the Chief Information Officer at some of Todd's parties. Warner was a roly-poly, red-faced man nearing the end of his career. Probably couldn't program his way out of a paper sack, but he knew enough to hire the kinds of nerds who could. What Warner could do was broker information, and for years he'd kept Todd gassed up with gossip on their sole corporate client.

"So, I promised you a heads-up. Here it is, okay? News you can use. Comin' at you!"

Hawk had been half-listening, but he drew himself to attention just in time to see Todd pull something shiny and round from his pocket. With a flick of his wrist, he let it sail. Hawk snatched it in midair, six inches from his nose. It was a big campaign button, the size of a coaster. The button was Telwest blue, and it bore a cryptic message: NSTS.

Hawk examined the button, turning it several directions. "Well, now, Todd, you've got me there. Seems to be some sort of acronym."

"It's the new, in-house motto. Button's coming out this week to Telwest employees, all 60,000 of 'em, in there with their paychecks. You know how they've all had to wear those badges with their rank in the organization?"

"As far as I know, they still do," Hawk said. "Number 1 for the top honchos, 2 for middle managers, 3 for line supervisors, 4 for the grunts at the bottom."

"Well, that's over," Todd declared. "Vern gave me the word. Now it's everybody wearing the same badge: NSTS for everyone."

"Which translates?" Hawk asked.

"'Nothing Stays the Same.' But keep that under your hat, okay? They'll have a contest for prizes in two weeks. Let the employees try and guess the slogan."

Hawk shook his head. "I know just the thing," he mumbled. "First prize, a two-day hunting trip to western Nebraska. Second prize, four days hunting. Third prize..."

There was a knock on the door, and Teresa swept in with two more pink slips. "This one's urgent," she said, then gasped as she flung down the messages. She wrinkled her nose, fanning the air as she ran from the room.

Todd shot a glance at the messages and scooted up to the edge of his chair. "Okay, here's the punch line. If it bleeds it leads, right? Well, there's gonna be blood-letting. Bottom line: the new CEO and his team are gonna cut the guts outta Telwest middle management. From now on, they'll recognize only two kinds of operations: profit centers and cost centers."

"And?" Hawk started to ask.

"That goes for everybody," Todd raced on. "Whether you're collecting quarters out of phone booths or you've got some hotshot new technology. You got a dynamite technology? Well, you better prove it works. And show 'em there's a market. That's what Vern says. He says there's another button coming out next month: M.O."

Hawk shrugged. "All I know is a Latin phrase: *modus operandi*."

Todd wagged his finger. "Gotta get more up to date, *amigo*. M.O. is 'market opportunity.' Vern says there's tons of opportunity out there, and as soon as Telwest gets right-sized, cuts out all their dead wood, he's gonna get me a..."

He stopped in midsentence and gave a knowing grin as he headed for the door. At the threshold, he stopped and spun around, waving his pink slips, gesturing with his messages. Now he wore a wide grin. "Lotta action these days. From POTS to PANS. Have you heard that one? From plain old telephone service to..."

"Pretty amazing new stuff," Hawk added. "Wally had it done up on a button of his own. I believe they all wear it at the video phone department."

"You like that? Marketing guy told me," Todd nattered on. "Oh, and one thing more. Matter of fact, that's what I came in to tell you. It seems they've hired a new VP for advanced technology. Name of Rowe. Granger Rowe. He said this guy's all business and he's out to clean house, fast.

"So, here's the punch line: no more nerds getting paid for noodling."

Hawk began to sense what was coming.

"He said they'll be out to find a poster child," Todd went on. "Some geek who's been playing with his zipper, diddling with some useless technology. The marketing guy says one product keeps coming up in their discussions. And one manager who's about to get the ax. Any guesses?"

Hawk shook his head, wide-eyed.

As Todd once again turned to leave, the euphoria of hunting was starting to fade, his grin tightening into a grimace. Todd peered at his partner and fairly hissed: "So, are you gonna call Wally?"

Hawk felt his own ire rising, the tension smoldering in his gut. There were times he wondered why he put up with all this. The speeches, Todd's simplistic advice. He knew he wasn't afraid of displeasing his partner. It was deeper than that. It was something about losing control.

As Hawk half-watched his partner framed in the doorway, a flurry of something caught his eye. It was back in the darkness of the hall, retreating toward the reception room. How much had Teresa heard? He wondered.

Now Todd was gone, and Hawk was in a world of his own again. But as he settled back in his desk chair, the intercom shattered the silence.

Teresa came on. "There's a call on line one." She was breathing hard. "It's for you, Hawk. Can you take it now? I'll put him through. It's Wally."

8

He'd lost some weight. Hawk could be sure of that, though he never looked at a scale. He had to have shed a few pounds, running off to the gym more than once to escape from the office. He could tell from the reaction of others. The looks he got out on the street. Women shifting their eyes in his direction. Men sizing him up before glancing away. His weight was back around 230 and he carried it well, suggesting the sculpted athlete beneath the doughball he'd let himself become.

Now he looked more like a classic car with a new paint job. A thirty-two-year-old-model. That was Hawk when he kept his weight off, and he felt the difference. Except for the weight he carried within. There was an incubus in his gut he could almost finger: a mass like a tumor, and he was pretty sure he knew what it was. Part of it was Wally Arneson. His one, sure client seemed about as secure as a trailer in a tornado.

It was late Friday afternoon as he headed over to the Wynkoop Brew Pub for his meeting with Wally: Happy Hour. Hawk felt anything but festive.

He hadn't told Todd about this meeting. That was the other load he was bearing. It had been two days since his partner had dropped by to give him a heads-up on Wally's situation. Todd had come by in his sweaty hunting gear before he'd even changed his clothes. Hawk might at least have reciprocated by filling him in on the meeting with their client. But he hadn't. Their relationship was unraveling.

It was a stunning September afternoon with a deep blue sky and shafts of sunlight streaming amber. But as Hawk trod through lower downtown, past the shiny green ficus trees and the mottled red brick buildings with bright awnings, he saw little of his surroundings.

Nearing the intersection of Wynkoop and 16th Streets, within a couple of blocks of the brew pub, the neighborhood was humming with life and buzzing signs in blaring neon: "Executive Tans," "The Oxygen Bar."

"Hey, watch it!" A hand shot out and grabbed his sleeve as he stepped off the curb, jerking him back to the sidewalk.

He looked up in time to see a light blue BMW careening around the corner, a convertible with the top down. As the car sped away, he noticed the license plate. It was the personalized kind that had originated in California. Now you could get them in Colorado. This one read: GET-IT-ALL.

Hawk glanced at his savior, a gray-haired man in a plaid woolen shirt.

"Wow, thanks!" he exclaimed. "I must have had my head out in space. Either that or up my career."

The man chuckled. "I know the feeling, or at least I can recall. See that warehouse over there across the street? Used to own it. Wholesale leather goods. Plenty of worries in that line o' work, I'll tell you."

"I can see it," Hawk said. "But it doesn't look like a warehouse now."

"Sold it just as soon as they started putting up the ballpark down on Blake Street. Whole thing's turned into condos. You can see the skylights."

"But you still come downtown?" Hawk asked.

"I do—come down and meet some of the old boys for lunch. When I feel like it, that is." The man waved as he went on. "Well, take it easy, son. Don't you worry, it'll work out. One way or another, it always does."

Well, maybe that was the way it works in a place like Denver. People reinvent themselves. One industry goes bust, another goes boom. He looked up at the Wynkoop, just ahead, remembered how the brew pub had been brought to life in an abandoned building by an unemployed geologist.

When the guy went looking for investors, his own mother had turned him down. But his old Little League coach had invested, and the geologist-turned-barkeep was off and running. He'd seen the future of Lower Downtown, before the new stadium had opened. Now Coors Field loomed on the near horizon—the red brick ballpark where, just this month, the Colorado Rockies had clinched a spot in the National League playoffs.

So, maybe that was the secret to succeeding in Denver. Always looking out over the horizon, never quite taking the world as it was. And it could be that was why he didn't quite fit in. It seemed he was always taking soundings in the here and now—probing for the resonance in things.

He watched an avalanche of up-and-comers tumbling out of sparkling cars, streaming into the Wynkoop. This was Friday afternoon on Casual Day, and there was a buzz in the crowd. Half of them in polyester warm-up suits of blazing orange and blue. Oh, happy day. Oh, happy hour.

Hawk glanced around the hoary old saloon but saw no sign of Wally. Strange. Wally was always on time. Beyond that, it seemed an odd place to meet for business, except Wally was like that. Sometimes he brought his crew of programmers down to the Wynkoop on a Friday afternoon for an exercise in team-building and elbow-bending.

There was a trade journal at the edge of the oaken bar, and Hawk picked it up. *Telecommunication Times*. He glanced at a couple of headlines:

- TECH INDUSTRIES BOOMING! CLIMBING TEN PERCENT PER ANNUM
- TELEPHONE BILLS IN U.S. GROWING FASTER THAN INFLATION

The crowd was feeling every bit of this good news. It was a loud crowd, but not aggressive. Usually there was a malcontent down at the end of a bar, trying to goad some guy into a fight. But not in this pub. The only angry voices were coming from the television mounted high on the aged brick wall. A lawyer bewailed the verdict in the O.J. Simpson trial. Newt Gingrich carried on about his Contract for America. Over the din, the politico was almost drowned out by the mournful sounds of Sheryl Crowe: "All I wanna do/do is have some fun..."

Hawk glanced at his watch. Still no sign of Wally. He flipped through the page of the trade journal, till a headline caught his eye: Granger Rowe Named to Top Spot in Technology at Telwest. "Rowe"—wasn't that the guy Todd had been going on about?

He put the article aside, looked around again and peered into the dark recesses of the bar, all the way down toward the dining area. That's when he saw him. Wally was coming in the back entrance and he was rotating his neck the way he did when he was nervous. His beacon head swept the Wynkoop back and forth in every direction until he spotted Hawk. With a half-smile, he jerked his head in greeting.

Hawk gave a start, as well. It was a shock of recognition.

There is a pallor that comes over some folks about the age of sixty, and it doesn't come slow. It falls like a shroud and envelopes them in aging, almost overnight. That was how he found Wally, and the sight of his client took him aback. Oh, he was the same guy. Had all his features, even most of his hair. But something about him seemed indistinct, diaphanous. He seemed a pale vestige of himself, like an overexposed photograph.

He couldn't believe how Wally had faded.

Hawk caught himself staring as he scraped back his bar stool and stood to greet him. Wally grinned as he held out his hand, and Hawk tried to smile. But the man's grip was like an ice pack. Hawk gave a jolt and hoped Wally hadn't noticed.

They stood at the bar as the bartender angled their glasses under the tap: pints of dark red LoDo Ale. Wally glanced at the trade journal Hawk had dropped on the counter while they waited for the thick heads of foam to settle.

"Tech industries booming," Wally read in a monotone, and Hawk thought he saw his neck quiver. Wally winced and took a quick step back from the bar. He jerked his head toward Hawk and looked him up and down. "Say, you're lookin' mighty trim there, Hawker. Been working out a little?"

"When I'm not chained to my desk on your do-good charitable projects," Hawk said. He considered showing him the article on Granger Rowe, but thought better of it. He folded the newspaper and stuck it in his back pocket instead.

Wally chuckled as he picked up his glass and plunked down ten dollars for the two of them. He swung his head around the tavern until he spotted an open table and nodded to Hawk. Slowly they made their way toward it.

As usual, on a Friday afternoon, the Wynkoop was a cacophony of disparate conversations. Sports fans in team gear shouted their loyalties. Many of them had come straight from work where the custom of dressing down was just taking hold. Thirty minutes ago they'd been on task, staring dutifully at computer screens. Closing out accounts for the week, filing travel reports. Now it was all "Raiders suck!" and "Go Broncos!"

But there was something else in the air. Hawk watched the denizens of the Wynkoop, sipping beer and hobnobbing, as he picked his way through the crowd. Moving closer, he began to recognize a murmur beneath the raucous cries, thrumming like a low chant. It was the buzz of business deals.

They passed a couple dressed in dark suits at a small table. The fellow was lining out figures on a legal pad as the woman nodded intently. Probably an upcoming trial or an investment deal. She smiled faintly as she moved in for a closer view. Her breasts strained against her tailored blouse. As they walked by, he thought he saw her hand slide underneath the table.

As they reached their table, Wally dropped into his chair and took a long draft of beer, draining half the pint with one swallow. He leaned back with a limpid smile. "Trim from the gym," he muttered absently and chortled. He stared at an elk head over the fireplace.

Hawk saw a row of whiskers Wally's razor had missed along his upper lip. Now a thin line of foam clung to it. He remembered that his wife had left. He sat and waited, noticed the big blue badge on the lapel of Wally's jacket. It had three bright yellow letters: AFR.

Hawk felt a jolt. He knew the jargon at Telwest and had heard about the button. It was something they made people wear in the last months of their employment. One last shot at finding another slot within the company: "Available for Reassignment."

Wally squinted at the elk and cocked his head, as though calculating the age of the animal or measuring its rack of antlers. Then, with a start, he lurched back toward his beer glass. He peered for a moment at the chestnut ale before seizing the glass in a desperate grasp and, in one swift motion, drained it.

Hawk watched as Wally swiveled his head, surveying

the room. He was twirling one finger in the air. "'Notha round," he muttered.

Hawk sat in silence. He had yet to take a sip from his glass. In his two professions, he'd learned two ways of dealing with people who drank under stress. As a journalist, you took advantage of situations like this, encouraging a guy to keep drinking if that's what it took to get at the truth. All the while questioning, probing. With a microcassette recorder under the table if possible. Listening was an adversarial skill in journalism.

Public relations, he'd found, was a different game. You had to perform more like a psychotherapist. You did nothing but listen. If a client was voluble and running off at the mouth, you listened, kept listening, and then listened some more. If the client was drinking, you let him go, although you never offered to buy the drinks. That was one way of keeping him coherent.

Before the fellow got too wasted, you pumped him for answers to a few basic questions. With whom do you want to communicate? What do you want to say? What do you want them to do? And, finally, what is it you want me to do for you? A related question, to be posed diplomatically, was this: How much are you willing to pay? You always got that figure and a signature beside it—if only on the back of a coaster from the bar.

After three or four minutes of twirling his finger, Wally rose to his feet. He stuck up an arm like a student waiting to recite in class. Hawk shuddered. This was not how you placed an order in a brew pub like the Wynkoop. You walked up to the bar. But now he was waving his arm, drawing glances from nearby tables.

Hawk looked aside as Wally clambered up from the table, then noticed he'd left something lying by his beer glass: a large manila envelope, filled to overflowing and open at the far end. Hawk couldn't see what was inside.

Wally sat back down and looked over at Hawk with a weary smile. "Finally caught her eye," he mumbled. "Another exercise in communication. Need a lot of that today, getting people to communicate. Some day, you know, they'll have a switch on the table. Flip a switch and buzz your waitress—simple as that. It'll revolutionize the industry."

Hawk had heard that before. It was the same idea a hamburger chain had come up with a decade ago. They'd had their booths all wired and you spoke your order into a microphone, like an indoor drive-in. The plan cut down on labor costs. But people missed being served by a smiling waitress, and the restaurants went bankrupt. Technology didn't always pan out.

He thought about sharing the story with Wally, but just then a twenty-something bar maid in a forest green sweatshirt ambled up to the table. She was a moderately attractive redhead with a body that sculpted the sweatshirt. There was an insignia in gold—Wynkoop—over her left breast.

"You waved?" she asked Wally with an impish smile. "Was it for me, or did you just want something from the bar?"

Wally swiveled in his chair 'til he was at eye level with the insignia. "Wynkoop," he said as he gave Hawk a wink. "Wynkoop—what a lovely name."

"Yeah, I know," the waitress cut in. "And what do you call the other one?'"

Wally motioned at the glasses and sputtered, "Fillerup," as he sank into spasms of laughter. "You hear that?" he asked Hawk as the waitress walked off. "'What do you call the other...'" He rocked in his chair, eyes tearing, relishing the joke. But as he reached toward his back pocket for a handkerchief, he clipped the big manila envelope with his elbow and it tumbled off the table.

A dozen blue buttons spilled out of the envelope and

rolled across the floor. Each of them looked just like Wally's. They all read "AFR."

For a split second, Wally peered at the buttons. Then his eyes went wide, aghast, as he dropped to his knees in a scramble to retrieve them. When he climbed back on his chair, his eyes were still wet. But not with tears of laughter.

Now Wally was weeping outright, his head in his hands, as he stared at the envelope that was back on the table, refilled with the buttons. Hawk sat and waited, remembering why he was there. He'd been hoping his client would share his agenda. Now he simply concentrated on his questions, ready to pose them when the time was right: "With whom do you want to communicate? What do you want to say?" But all the while his stomach was starting to bubble.

The waitress came back with two more ales, but Wally didn't see her. Hawk handed her ten dollars and motioned to put the beers on the table. He took another sip from his first glass. Disciplined, he reviewed the questions he was there to ask: "With whom do you want..."

Till the tension escalated and his stomach felt like fire. Finally, he could take no more. "Wally, for God's sake, I know what AFR means!" A table of Bronco fans swung 'round from their beers and looked toward him.

"Wally, it's Available for Reassignment. Look here. Look at me! Now, who are the other buttons for? And how long do we have before they fire you?"

There are a couple of guidelines for getting personal information from a nerd, and Hawk knew at once he had violated both of them. First was that you never addressed personal matters directly; you talked about something like work first. Second, you never raised your voice. Realizing he had done the unthinkable, along with abandoning the public relations questions he was there to ask, Hawk took a deep breath and tried an end run.

"So, how goes the programming, Wally? Last I heard, you were trying to work up an address book for the video phone."

There was only silence, as Wally stared into his beer. Hawk sat and waited, steeped in dread. How could he have cast off his professional role and hollered at his client that way? It was the same failing that had haunted him all his life. He'd give himself rules: certain questions to ask, principles to follow.

Keep your weight low.

Hands inside the opponent's shoulder pads.

Block and spin ...

The rules were a comfort, even if they sometimes felt confining. A person could define himself by what he did, the precision of it. What did it matter if he was a *pastiche* of racial features, an ethnic enigma? People stopped asking, "What are you?" They only paid attention to what you did.

But then there came a moment when he'd bust outside the rules—exploding in anger to leg-whip an opponent, blowing up at Wally. Had his client heard that? "How long do we have before you lose your job?"

Hawk was sweating. He took a long draught of beer, draining the first glass as he reached for the second. He took a new tack. "How'd the programmers do this week, Wally? How many lines of code?"

Wally gave a shudder and took a sip of beer. It was another minute or so before he spoke, in a low and throaty voice Hawk hadn't heard from him before. "That's not what it's about," he muttered.

"I'm not sure I got that."

"It isn't about the technology," Wally went on. "Not really. That's not what the video phone means. I figured that out last year, when Martha left. Went out one night and never came back. I tell you, it took me by surprise—just shocked me."

He stopped to lift his beer glass, set it down with a shudder. Hawk was afraid he'd heard the last from Wally. But then he went on.

"See, I sat up there at my desk all day, and what did I have left? I spent a lot of time just ogling the mountains."

"And what did you have left?" Hawk asked.

"Oh, there was Gladys, the Office Mom—every now and then, when her husband would believe she was working late. And... and then I had the programmers."

Wally glanced at the envelope, bulging with buttons. His shoulders quivered and again he began to cry. Hawk knew who the buttons were for. It was Wally who'd have to break the news to Gladys and the programmers.

Hawk stood and waved at the bar maid, holding up two fingers. She saw him and returned in a few minutes with the frothing mugs. "Hey, you're a big one, aren't you? Hard to miss. Notice I didn't ask you, 'Got a big one?'"

Hawk smiled slightly but held up a cautionary hand. As she set down the beers, the waitress glanced at Wally. She turned away with a sympathetic frown.

"Say, she's full of 'em," Wally sniffled, his head in his hands. 'Got a big one.' That's all right. Real live wire and not bad-looking, all that red hair. But what do you suppose she'd be like if you got to know her better?"

"I can't imagine," Hawk said. "I've only heard a few of her one-liners."

"I'll tell you what. They're all alike." He looked aside and shook his head. "One on one, they want it all." Wally took a long draw on his new beer and fell silent.

Hawk sat and thought about his own athletic history with women. It seemed they were always around and not much of an aggravation if he didn't stay too long with any one of them. But constant turnover had its drawbacks. After a while, their flesh began to feel like warmed-over chicken, or a melon in the sun. In time, he considered, they all felt pretty much the same.

He wondered what it might be like for a scrawny guy like Wally. He'd have to work harder at his sex life. Would there be any fun in it? A thrill in the chase?

"So, there you have it," Wally said softly, "the future of the video phone."

"How's that again?"

But that was the last coherent statement out of Wally. Perhaps it was the beers, although he'd only had a couple. Or, maybe technoids were like clams. They opened up only when the tide was right. Could be that was a third theorem when trying to get any sort of honest information out of them. Get it while you can.

As he worked on his beer, Wally started nattering on about who it was he wanted to communicate with and what he wanted to say. He seemed to regain a spark of confidence. He sat up with his shoulders squared, and made some mention of a plan. But mostly he was spouting advertising slogans of the telecommunications industry.

"Plug in to your neighbor," he'd exclaim. "Hook up with your friends." Now and then he gestured around the brew pub, pointing out people with whom he might like to make contact, perhaps to interest them in a video phone. By and large, they seemed to be young, buxom women.

"But what for?" Hawk asked him, suggesting some direction for their conversation. "What good is a video phone? What would they do with it?"

Wally would give a vague smile, swivel his head around the bar, and mutter some bromide. "Find a friend at hand."

Client or no, it was a waste of time to carry on like this. Hawk had plans for the weekend. He fumbled for a business card to hand it to Wally. If he couldn't do any work for him, at least he could remind him who the hell he was. It might prove helpful when he sent him an invoice for a billable hour, albeit if it might turn out to be the last one.

But as he started to leave, he noticed that Wally had changed his demeanor. The man had swiveled around in his chair. He was sitting bolt upright, staring toward the door.

Hawk got up quietly and stepped back into the shadows of an alcove at the back of the brew pub. If he couldn't get anything out of talking with Wally, perhaps he could learn something by watching him.

Hawk followed his gaze, scanning the entrance to the Wynkoop. In the last rays of late afternoon, it was hard to see through the blue cloud over the bar, the one area where they let patrons light up.

Then he saw her.

Slowly, the phantasm of a stylish woman came into view. It was hard to make her out against the mahogany walls, for she was almost dark as the décor. In a mottled blouse, black on russet, she seemed to meld with the woodwork. But as she came into focus, Hawk picked up on her skin tone. It was vibrant and glowing, a kind of high bronze he'd seldom seen before. It was a stunning shade, the kind of compound that comes of races mixing well. He looked down at the back of his own hand and considered his complexion—nondescript, dusty, mudlike.

She was a lithe young woman, strong and slender, as she strode across the bar. Her hair was black as anthracite, tumbling down over her shoulders. It was the color of dark Africa, but thick and scarcely curled. She might have passed for East Indian, but for the full lips and broad nostrils. That and her elegant cheekbones. Cherokee? Lakota?

As she looked around, she spotted Wally and gave him a warm, open smile. Hawk watched her come up to the table as Wally got to his feet. The man was staring holes through her. Then her eyes narrowed slightly. She seemed to hold Wally's gaze, still half-smiling.

It was then Hawk noticed a last detail. There was an added fold of flesh at the edges of her eyes. Hawk could see how the feature rounded her face and deepened her smile, and then he truly wondered if he could believe his eyes. Another Nanticoke?

As the woman greeted Wally, she said, "Cassandra Harmon." Hawk gave a start. He recognized that surname, had heard it a lot at Haskell. Then, somewhere in the back of his mind, the tumblers stopped spinning and fell into place. The intern he'd applied for, the marketing major. They'd sent her straight to Wally at Telwest.

Cassandra clasped Wally's hand in both of her own and kept him standing for a moment. As she leaned forward, Hawk heard her tell him something strange. "Scotch-Irish, with a dash of Scandinavian."

Wally said, "Huh?"

"That would be your ancestry. Did I get it right?"

He shrugged and shook his head. "Uh, maybe so, but why..."

"Oh, I like to guess. I could see you trying to figure out mine."

9

Hawk had paused for a moment, somewhat taken by this Cassandra. But he'd slipped out a door at the back of the alcove as soon as she and Wally started talking. It seemed that voyeurism had its limits. And, besides, he had plans. It was the weekend. He was headed for the mountains.

He stopped by the office long enough to check for phone messages, and as he plopped down in his desk chair he felt the trade journal in his back pocket. He pulled it out and turned on his desk lamp. He thumbed back to the article on Granger Rowe.

It didn't take long to read, a typical in-house public relations puff piece. The obligatory love feast whenever they hired a new executive. "He's an emblem of the new Telwest," the CEO announced. "An 'intrapreneur.' A change agent in the new economy."

For his part, Rowe allowed as how he was excited as well. It was something about "the thrill of an industry in revolution." He said he was "ecstatic" for the opportunity to introduce "breakthrough technologies for a new tomorrow." He didn't mention what technologies those might be.

Hawk could read the subtext. Telwest was sending a message to investors. They were open for business, no more hidebound public utility. He knew part of the purpose was seasonal. If September meant the start of football season, it also spelled the end of the third quarter for stock returns. The rumor was that Telwest was "missing its targets," not "making the quarter." September was a good month for injecting a little good news.

Still, Wally aside, the whole business bored him. So Granger Rowe was bent on making all things new. So what? It was the same, sad jangle of the boom on the horizon, the rhythm of a city that couldn't fnd its beat.

He turned off his desk lamp and sat in the dark.

An ex-geologist named Natalie owned a small condominium near Steamboat Springs, a few hours outside Denver, and now and then she'd invite him to come up. It was not a fervid relationship. Although she was a reasonably attractive woman about his own age, Hawk had about as much in common with Natalie as a broadcast journalist with a newspaper reporter.

But Natalie was an easy person to visit for a weekend, if you needed nice surroundings and a little carnal comfort. She had lost her career as a data analyst in Denver when the oil industry crashed ten years before. With no other jobs in sight, she'd headed for the mountains where she found work as a desk clerk in a ski resort. Now she was something like the manager of front desk operations, as near as Hawk could remember, and the job kept her busy into the early evenings.

Hawk liked that. He'd taken up snowshoeing and would be off in the woods all day, arriving just in time to greet Natalie as she got off work. After a few pleasantries and a couple of beers, they'd be out of their skivvies and into the sack. Then it was down to the lodge for drinks and dinner with the après ski crowd and back to her place for a full night under a warm comforter.

He thought about Natalie as he drove along the twisting highway through the dark pines and stark, gray mountains. For a while, he tried to remember how the two of them had met, and then he gave that up when he discovered that he couldn't.

He stopped for coffee in a town called Granby that seemed increasingly hard to find. There were housing developments going up throughout the wooded hills on the outskirts—starter castles on multi-acre lots—and a new supermarket with a glistening, black asphalt parking lot that took up half the main street. But he found a small, log-covered café a half-block down a side street. Through the window, he spotted what he was looking for: coffee in big, steaming mugs and cinnamon rolls dripping with white sugar frosting.

There was a pine-covered wall where rows of mugs hung on wooden pegs, and the mugs were inscribed: Gordo, Bert, Marge, and Lefty. Hawk took a seat at one end of the lunch counter and watched the Saturday morning crowd assemble. One by one, the locals stumbled in to the café, exhaling clouds of frosty air from outdoors. As they grabbed their mugs and helped themselves to coffee, they crowded around tables and jostled into booths that lined the wall. There was a warm glow to the banter and laughter that must have been going on for decades, and Hawk let it seep into him and warm him.

On the road again, he was sorry to find his real life returning. Slowly, the bonhomie of the café began to fade and he found himself facing off against some major league concerns. Right now, the highway was clear enough. But by late tomorrow it'd be a parking lot all the way from Berthoud Pass into the city as the skiers crawled back to their desk jobs.

He told himself to just enjoy the day. The sun was sparkling on a blanket of snow that had fallen overnight, and he was sure the storm had dumped a load of it on Steamboat. It would be a wonderful day to strap on his snowshoes and retreat deep into the woods.

But soon other worries crowded his mind. He'd stayed long enough the night before to see that his client seemed to settle down in the presence of one Ms. Harmon. Still, would Wally really come back to his senses?

And the intern. When he'd filled out the application form, he'd envisioned the kind of person Haskell would send them: some kid who'd completed a major in economics along with a summer's worth of business experience in a snow-cone stand.

But this Cassandra seemed older than that. And assertive! She'd gotten Wally's attention in a way Hawk never had. Just nailed him to the wall. The bottom line was that if she knew something about marketing, he'd damn well better get along with her. Wally had mentioned something about a plan. Well, even if he came up with a way to turn a profit on the video phone, he had maybe two months. That was the typical stay of execution for a Telwest manager wearing an AFR badge. When it came to line workers like the programmers, the ax could fall even in a matter of days. How much time ...

Suddenly, a flash of brown and black and white came hurtling toward the highway. Hawk flinched and hit the brakes as a deer bounded out of the trees. It was a young doe, frozen in fear, only a few feet in front of him. Hawk stared at the animal, wide-eyed, as the brakes screeched. He skidded to a stop just shy of the animal. He leaned on the horn, his heart pounding. But the doe stood in place, gazing into his eyes through the windshield. For a minute she peered at the car, drawing breaths in rhythmic gasps, just as he was. The two of them seemed locked in place, breathing to a silent drum. Then, with a start, she turned in her tracks and loped away.

Hawk sat in the car for several minutes and tried to collect his thoughts. Something about his work. But it was gone, and he couldn't recall.

Natalie raised up on an elbow to peer at the clock. Hawk cracked an eyelid and watched a flaccid breast emerge from beneath the flannel sheets. He shut his eyes and slunk beneath the covers.

"I'm starving, and no wonder?" Natalie announced. She had adopted the recent custom of framing statements as questions, and Hawk flinched. It was a practice that didn't make any sense to him. He'd never understood why people fell into speaking that way. Natalie might have wondered, too, had she given thought to what she was doing. But she seldom did. Natalie took her cues from the crowd.

"So what time is it, Natalie? I can't see from here."

"Seven fifteen, and you can take your time, big fella. I'll just bet you're tired. That tromping through the woods and then, my, all that pile driving."

Hawk grimaced as Natalie gave a snicker. In addition to her knobby body and habit of stating facts as questions, her constant use of geological terms for sexual functions got on his nerves. Everything was "deep drill," "slant hole," "slurry," and she'd give out with a guffaw at every earthy witticism.

Her problem was that she'd spent too long in a jock profession, Hawk thought. After graduating from the Colorado School of Mines, for years she'd dated only exploration geologists. Even married one for a time. And a rank, redneck bunch like that could get to you, he decided.

Still, she was the only woman he knew in Steamboat and he loved coming up to the Routt National Forest. The afternoon had been mystical, deep in the woods, with the last, light flakes of the snowstorm falling. As the late rays of sunlight began to fade, the forest had gone totally silent. Then he'd heard a twig snap and turned to see a huge, regal moose treading through the snow.

At times like those, he suspected he might be religious, though not in any Christian sense—their one Creator who was somehow responsible for all the good and all the evil in the universe. What he thought he believed in was a pair of gods from the Nanticoke tradition: Manito, who gave life, and Okee, who destroyed it. He recognized two spirits like that within himself. Usually they were in combat.

Now he found himself praying, as the shadows of late afternoon stole deep into the forest. If he could ever learn to reconcile those spirits inside him, get them in balance.

He got to the condo at dusk, and Natalie was in the shower. She'd set out two beers on the nightstand and hollered a scabrous one-liner as she heard the front door slam. Something about his big drill bit, and she asked him to bring in a towel.

"And this is Hawk? He's my friend from Denver?"

They were sitting at one end of a massive, mahogany bar that coursed along one wall of the ski lodge. The opposite wall was all fireplace—a huge, graystone construction that loomed above a lounge of Navajo rugs and leather couches. A crackling fire cast a rosy glow around the place, and the room was redolent with an aroma of burning piñon logs.

For some time, tourism studies had shown that half the visitors to Colorado ski resorts were like Hawk. They didn't ski. So the best resorts had invested heavily in amenities for the aprés ski market. The lodge at Steamboat gave the appearance of a turn of the century luxury hotel, but in fact it had been built to look like that only three years before, in 1992.

The far wall was taken up by a two-story window that ran from floor to ceiling, between the fireplace and bar. One could look out at the mountain and see a good part of the intermediate ski run—the skiers at the top like smudges scarcely moving against the alabaster snow, swerving down and down till they burst into the floodlights at the bottom of the slope in reds and greens, and lavenders and yellows: a kaleidoscope of swirling, incandescent colors.

At one side of the ski slope was an area for snowboarders—the newest trend in the mountains. For a minute, he watched that crowd. They were younger and more boisterous, sometimes threatening to crash into one or another of the skiers. They dressed differently, too: dark sweatshirts and jackets, almost a Gothic look.

Hawk pulled back from the spectacle and tried to attend to what Natalie was saying. "And, Hawk, this is Brad, and Kevin? And Russell tending bar?"

He shook hands all around, half-wondering how many of these guys had occupied his spot between the flannel sheets in Natalie's wood-paneled bedroom.

Russell was a slight, spindly fellow, maybe forty, with a bushy handlebar mustache. He wore a button-down shirt with a bow tie and red suspenders. Somehow he looked out of place as a bartender, like a refugee from some other profession. There was a ruckus down at the other end of the bar and, as Russell went down to look in on a gaggle of snowboarders, Natalie told him that was so.

"He's a lawyer?" she told him. "And Todd, over there, was a stockbroker? And Kevin, he's some kind of PhD?" She said Steamboat had acquired so many displaced white-collar professionals out of Denver that they'd started a Great Books group and a chapter of the Mensa Society.

Something about what she said struck a chord in Hawk. In an instant, he felt a knot come loose in his head with a great rush of euphoria. He set down his beer and looked up high. It almost seemed he could see his spirits soaring past the fireplace all the way to the beams of the ceiling. He shook his head and laughed as he saw Natalie quizzically peering at him.

If Wally was let go, if Telwest folded—well, what the hell? There would always be these ski resorts. Why couldn't he come up and tend bar and write novels, hang out with guys like Russell and the rest?

He was about to ask Natalie about others who were up here when a loud noise erupted at the far end of the bar. It was the snowboarders: three spindly teenagers with high, scratchy voices and the latest street profanity.

"Hey, motha-fucka!" One of them was face to face with Russell. He was reaching over the bar, grabbing the bartender's suspenders.

"Watch what you're saying," Russell told him. He had a strong, lawyer's voice but it was quavering. "I told you, I need to see some identification."

"ID, my ass. I'll draw my own beer," another retorted. He motioned to the other two, and the three of them hiked over to a hinged panel in the center of the counter. The first kid flipped up the wooden panel and stepped behind the bar. His two friends followed.

Hawk watched the trio take their first few steps. There were two or three other couples at the bar—pale as Russell—also looking on. At first, he thought about giving the kids a warning. But something was stirring down around his solar plexus. The same, dark energy that lurked there all the time. Now, the spirit gathered force as it snaked up through his intestines. He felt his mind go numb as the anger flared and he lost control of his body. From this point on, he knew he was only along for the ride.

A leg kicked out and cleared away two bar stools. Then, with two strides, Hawk was vaulting over the bar. As he hurtled through the air, he clipped one of the snowboarders in the back of the head with a cleated boot, caught the other in a kidney with his knee. The teenagers screamed and tumbled to the floor. Hawk grasped each of them by the back of the collar and shoved them in the face of the third kid. "Second call, dudes," he snarled. "Anyone for IDs?"

In a matter of seconds, the snowboarders were out the

door. There was a smattering of applause around the lodge as Russell poured Hawk a fresh beer. The couple at the bar proposed a toast. But the euphoria was gone.

Natalie was shaking her head. "Lots of folks come up to get out of the rat race," she was saying. "But, you know what? The rats know their way here, too."

"There's only one physical requirement for most of these jobs," Russell added. "You have to have a thick skin."

That night, Hawk couldn't sleep. The scene at the bar kept playing in his head. He couldn't believe how he'd lost control. How Okee, the evil one, had won. He got up about midnight and padded out to the living room. He turned on the TV and surfed through the channels till he came across a skin flick—some college girls flinging off their ski duds and warming one another up in a hot tub. It was pretty hot stuff, as the squealing gave way to bona fide moans. The caption read The Summit Group. Wasn't that the outfit that owned this resort?

He thought about something Natalie had said, how she'd been told to hire the best looking candidates for jobs she could find. They all submitted photos and someone from the Summit Group reviewed the applications. "Some of these kids can barely process a credit card," she'd said. "But that doesn't seem to bother the execs. It's like they have a different agenda."

The film was titillating, but Hawk soon began to lose interest in the nubile breasts and bare bottoms. He couldn't clear his mind of the bar scene. He got up and got dressed and left Natalie a note. He headed back to Denver.

10

"Strangled in the cradle, eh? Hell of a way to start a new career." Art Branscomb gave a dark chuckle as he reached across the Formica table for two packets of sugar and a container of cream. They were sitting in the snack bar in the basement of the *Chronicle*. It was a detour from Hawk's customary route to work, but he'd tried to grab Art before the man's cocktail hour started at lunchtime.

"Well, that wasn't the whole purpose of the trip."

Branscomb snorted as he stirred the cream and sugar into syrupy concoction that looked more like a mixed drink than coffee. "No, I guess not," he said. "I imagine it was your passion for that... what's her name? You'll forgive me if I can't keep all the players straight." Some granules of sugar had spilled onto the table, and they clung to a sleeve of his faded corduroy jacket. With his tousled, gray hair and plaid shirt, Art could have passed as a college prof no less than a psychiatrist-turned-columnist.

Hawk thought a minute. "That could be right. Maybe a change is what I had in mind all along. You know how it feels to get up in the mountains."

"Well, there's nothing wrong with a little re-careering. Look at me, from a doc-in-a-box shrink to an ink-stained hack on a daily fish wrap. People change when they find a new direction. But you, my friend, you're all over the map. Down to the Broncos, up to the mountains. You ever hear that old Ukrainian proverb? 'If you don't know where you're going, any road will take you there.'"

Branscomb turned to his coffee cup. He took a swizzle stick and stirred up all the sugar and cream in it. Then he threw his head back and gulped it down like a straight shot. He shuddered and glanced at his watch. Four hours till lunch at the Press Club.

Hawk watched closely as Branscomb went on. "These are dangerous times. No telling what people will do to keep their jobs. I've seen it. But you're a craftsman, Hawk. Not just a *schmoozer* like that tinhorn partner of yours. You've got your craft. You know what you're doing and you care about it. Am I right?"

Hawk sat in silence. Almost imperceptibly, he nodded.

Branscomb looked at Hawk with an inquisitive smile. "Do you know what the word *kroft* means in German? Ever heard that? It means 'power!'"

That insight seemed to follow him outside, as the morning came powerfully alive. It was a gorgeous September day, and the sun shown bright through the last, dark golden leaves that had weathered the early snowstorm. In his hiking boots from the night before, he made his way through the canyons of concrete in the financial district. Striding along 17th Street, he came upon the tall Telwest building where Wally and his video phone department hung out. At least, where they'd worked last week. When he got to the office, what would he find?

For the moment, he found, he didn't much care. Branscomb's counsel always had a dark side, a hint of bad omens. But the talk had cleared his mind. And the outing in the mountains had his capillaries expanding. The clear, cold air kept pumping inside him, and it seemed to spread his head. Once again his thoughts turned to Manito, the Giver of

Life, who always received the first fruits of the harvest. Not to deny the insidious Okee, sowing seeds of destruction. But on a day such as this it was hard not to believe that Manito was alive and at work in the universe.

Soon he was deep in the historic, red-brick warehouses of Lower Downtown. He rounded the corner on Blake Street and bounded up the weathered granite stairs to the Hermitage, ready for the day.

But as he swung open the oak door to the big musty building, he quickly sensed something was wrong. There were no lights on in his suite of offices. On the first day of the work week, the place was dark as coal.

Hawk pulled out his keys and unlocked the door, flipped on the green banker's light that sat on the reception desk. The desktop was bare, except for a somber, legal-looking document with a note scrawled on a Post-it.

> Hawk,
>
> Something just came up and I'll be out all morning. High-level confab with my buddy Vern Warner, the CIO at Telwest. He's been talking with the new VP for Advanced Technologies—this Granger Rowe. All kinds of new technologies, market opportunities. Vern says the field's wide open. Wow! Rowe wants some new products out there, like yesterday. Anyway, Vern might be hot for the video phone. So, have you been in touch with Wally?
>
> Oh—here's our lease agreement for next year. You need to sign.
>
> Todd
>
> P.S. I haven't seen Teresa.

Hawk picked up the contract and scanned it. A year's lease: he'd forgotten it was coming due. Together with utilities, Teresa's salary, the health insurance, and God knows what more. Well, there'd be no problem on his end as long as Wally played his part: the geek that lays the golden egg. But...

The phone rang. He reached to pick it up then let it go. There was something about lacking a receptionist that spoke too clearly of a business going under. It rang four times then the answering machine clicked on.

"Hullo, Hawk? It's Wally. Say, there's somebody I want you to meet. Short notice, I know, but I hope you can make it. Ten o'clock this morning at the Starbucks, corner of 16th and Blake. Sorry I can't come—got all this damn programming—but she'll find you.

"Oh, yeah. I've got your work authorization form from Telwest. Two months is all we can hire you for, see if we can do something with the video phone. Gotta run. See ya."

Two months? That's all? Hawk lunged for the phone, but he was too late. Wally was off the line. He set the lease back on the desk, staring at it. A twelve-month commitment on the lease, a client committing to two.

The phone rang a second time. Where the hell was Teresa? This time he picked it up. "Mountain High Communications."

"Hawk? Oh I'm so glad I caught you. It's Teresa."

Hawk said, "Hey, it doesn't sound like you. Are you all right?"

"*Si, si*, but I'm glad you can't see me. I've been up half the night with little Ricky. He's been coughing so hard now he's spitting up blood. Gotta take him to the doctor. You know my sister usually covers for me..."

"Sure, I remember. Your sister, Maria..."

"*Claro*. But last night she and Carlos, they had such a fight. I been telling her, 'You stay with him. You wanta end up a single parent, like me? You guys got two paychecks. You stay there, no matter what.' But now I just..."

Hawk had never heard Teresa carry on this way. There was an aura she projected around the office that he now recognized for what it was—professional patina, an overlay on the gritty realities of her other life. Under the stress of a sick child and her sister's domestic conflicts, she sounded like she was coming undone.

"Well, listen, Teresa. I'll manage here. You go to the doctor and take care of your son. Call me later in the day and let me know how he's..."

"Oh, thank you, Hawk. *Gracias a Dios.* I just thank God every day—for you and that I have this job. If I didn't have the benefits, what would I do? *Si, si,* Hawk. I'll call you." And she was off the line.

Hawk glanced at his watch. It was thirty minutes till his appointment at ten o'clock. Should he try to get some work done? He walked back to his office, reached for the light switch. Then he waved off the notion and settled into his chair. For a half-hour he sat in the darkness with Wally and Teresa. The worlds they inhabited. *En cada cabeza es un mundo.* He had a sense of some dark force, pulling them into the same orbit. Would he be drawn into that vortex? He couldn't tell. He listened to the rhythm of their voices.

At 9:55 Hawk roused himself and trotted over to Starbucks. He stepped inside a couple of minutes late and blinked, coming in from the bright sunlight. As he adjusted to the surroundings, he surveyed the room.

The coffee bar was abuzz with its customary assortment of caffeine addicts. Here and there a gaggle of well-dressed women, taking a break from the galleries and gift shops of lower downtown. There were other kinds of leisurites, with even more time to kill. Some elderly retirees, nursing a single cup of coffee throughout the morning while thumbing through a book from the Tattered Cover or the latest scandal-laced edition of *Westword,* Denver's free newspaper. Others wore the plaid shirts and weathered faces of laid-off workers from the oil business. They sat staring into space.

But, mostly, there was a sea of blue-suited business mongers, leaning on tables cluttered with their lattés, crowding over marked-up legal pads.

"What was it you said?" they all seemed to be asking. "How's that again?" There's an edge to the cacophony of a coffee bar, and it's there by design, Hawk decided. The buzz is in the bedlam. It's not just the caffeine that heightens your senses. It's the strain of trying to hear what's being said.

Wally had said he'd be meeting a "she." Hawk had a good idea who that would be, but if it was the intern, Cassandra, he had to be careful not to appear to recognize her. He lowered his head and looked around as he contemplated a three-dollar slice of carrot cake to complement his coffee. The cake looked delicious, stocked with raisins and nuts and slathered in white icing. But three bucks?

Then he spotted her at one of the rear tables, and quickly averted his eyes. He stepped up to the counter, about to order, when he felt a touch at his elbow.

"Let me get that, Hawk Kidree."

He looked down at Cassandra. Although long accustomed to being picked out in a crowd and approached by strangers, he stopped for a moment, taken aback. Up close, she was even more striking than when he'd spied on her in the Wynkoop on Friday afternoon. She was wearing a mustard yellow turtleneck under a forest green woolen pants suit. A stone pendant with a Native American profile hung from a braided leather cord around her neck. He recognized the logo of Haskell University, carved in stone. The whole outfit lit sparks off her bronze complexion and brilliant black hair.

Hawk pulled himself together. "Maybe you'd better wait to see what all I have my eye on. That carrot cake is a month's salary, but it looks pretty good. And ... do I know you?"

She avoided the question as she pulled in line behind him, leaned toward him with a winsome smile. "You order anything that appeals to you." I'm Cassandra Harmon. Wally told me what you looked like, but he needn't have bothered."

Hawk wasn't sure what that meant, but he let it pass. He ordered a supergrande coffee of the day and the carrot cake. He let her lead the way to the table where she'd been sitting, following behind.

Hawk sipped his coffee and launched into the cake. He waited for her to say something, but she sat silent. Whenever he glanced up, he noticed the same winsome smile, although she quickly turned serious when she saw she was being observed.

He waited for her to open the conversation with some sort of agenda, but instead she suddenly stared at him and flashed a piercing frown. "What do you keep looking at?" she demanded. "My eyes?"

"More like the corners of your eyelids. Have you ever noticed them?"

"Jesus, are you another one? Look, I was born with a lot of strange parts and odd features. Do I pay them any mind? No. And I hate being stared at."

She paused, and then she asked, "Don't you?"

Hawk finished the last dollop of frosting from the carrot cake and took a big swallow of his coffee. "All right, then, here we are. I guess Wally sent you."

She sat in silence, as did he. All around them, the business of a Monday morning coffee bar droned like a chorus of jacked up cicadas.

Finally, he said, "Look, Cassandra. This is not my favorite place to try to carry on a conversation. Why don't we go back to my office—it's just a couple of blocks from here—and we'll start over."

She said nothing, but nodded and followed him out the

door. As they walked along outdoors, she stayed behind him, single file. At the Hermitage, Hawk flicked on the lights of his office suite and led his guest back to his office. He left her there while he put on some coffee, then returned to his desk. He sat down and looked at her impassively and listened to the silence.

Finally, she spoke. "Do you know who I am?"

He paused for a moment. "You're a very attractive young woman, probably tri-racial, but you act like an Indian. You seem to like silence, and you walk single file. Your name is Cassandra something. You're wearing a pendant from Haskell All Nations University, which happens to be my *alma mater*. I have an idea you might be a Nanticoke, like me. That's why I was looking at you intently. And you like to ask a lot of questions. It might be a way of controlling a conversation, or maybe it's just your style."

She gave a cautious smile. "And do you know what I'm doing here?"

"Maybe it's your turn now. You'd better tell me."

"Well, I am from Haskell. I'm a recent grad, a marketing major, and I've been sent to work with Wally Arneson. It's a two-month assignment, on the video phone. I'd thought you might be expecting me. There was a form that came from Telwest and your name was on it. And, of course, I recognized your name." Again, she gave a knowing smile.

Another closet football fan, thought Hawk, groaning within. But it seemed there was something more to this woman. He didn't quite get her smile. It was somewhat enigmatic: not so much seductive as the kind of warm expression you might get from a close acquaintance. And she looked a bit mature for a recent graduate; he'd noticed that the first time he'd seen her interact with Wally.

"So, what can I do for you?" he asked.

She took a note pad out of her briefcase. "Maybe you could tell me what you know about Telwest," she said.

Hawk got up and poured them each some coffee. Then he leaned back in his chair. He put his feet up on the desk and, for the next half-hour, scoured his brain for every gram of fact he could come up with. He was surprised, in fact, to find out how much he had to say. This was the kind of conversation he ought to have had with Todd, had he ever been able to set him down for a spell.

"Well, it goes back to the divestiture of AT&T, ten years ago," he began. "Do you know about that, how they created the Baby Bells—Telwest and the seven others?"

"A little bit," she said, taking notes intently.

"There was a sudden flood of technology after they broke up the AT&T system. Pent-up technology that had been on the shelf for a long time. You see, that always had been one of the arguments for breaking up AT&T: that there was lots more than the monopoly had been willing to deliver."

Hawk went into the difficulties faced by the regional phone companies, being forced to open their markets to all sorts of competitors for one thing. He was afraid he might be boring her, but she gave no sign of losing interest. Must be used to taking notes in lectures, he decided.

"But that wasn't the greatest challenge," he went on.

She looked up with an expectant smile and he felt a sudden shiver. What was that about? It was the smile, he decided, and the fact that he wasn't accustomed to talking this much.

"The big thing was having to change their culture from a regulated monopoly to an aggressive competitor," he said. "And, add to that, the market was constantly changing." Hawk described the badges the employees had had to wear. And he told her about one of Wally's experiences.

"So one night, they were at a crucial phase of developing the video phone. And he decides to go back and work on his prototype, a little midnight engineering. But he couldn't get in his office. It seems Telwest had always had a policy of locking down the elevators at six p.m."

"That doesn't sound like any way to compete in a business like telecom," Cassandra commented.

"It wasn't, and it isn't. The Baby Bells are losing something like seven percent of their traditional revenue stream every year," Hawk answered. "If they're going to avoid constant layoffs, they have to come up with new products to offer."

"Like the video phone," Cassandra said.

"Well, maybe," Hawk said. "But how much do you know about it?"

"Quite a bit, I guess. They had me do some research before I came over here. So, I can tell you what I know. But, hey, it's 11:30. Is there a place you like to eat? Why don't we do it over lunch?"

Hawk found himself puzzled as they made their way to I. B. Wau's, a new Chinese restaurant in lower downtown. He had plenty of questions about this Cassandra, but it was impossible to pose them to someone walking two steps behind him. She didn't behave like an intern, for one thing. Oh, sure, she asked good questions and took notes. But she also seemed to take charge—not in a bossy way, more like an equal. He wondered if she'd try to pay for lunch.

Beyond that, something about her seemed vaguely familiar. She reminded him of someone he'd known. As a child, not an adult. He let his mind probe a few of the images that came up.

There was a girls' basketball game. Had he watched it? No he'd been the ref. When he was a college student back in Kansas. A little point guard, maybe twelve years old. That kid couldn't shoot a lick—couldn't throw it in the ocean—but she could handle the ball like she owned it, taking charge, dribbling through the opposition. The kind of girl who'd maybe grown up with older brothers.

There was something else about that game. As they approached the restaurant, he tried to recall. It was a fight, that was it. Little junior high girls, he'd never thought it possible. But this kid—she was tied up by another player, and she wouldn't let go. Not even when Hawk blew his whistle. When her opponent finally wrested the ball away, she took a step back and hit her in the jaw. Just hauled off and floored her with a haymaker.

Hawk gave a quick glance back over his shoulder. Was he making this up? No, there was one thing more, about where she'd run off. After the kid had been thrown out of the game, he'd found her …

But it wouldn't come back; he couldn't remember. Why was he having these flashbacks?

He opened the door for Cassandra, but she stood still out on the sidewalk, waiting to follow him. Squinting in the sunlight, he glanced at her again. Then he closed the door and stepped back outside, looking more intently. She was smiling in that knowing way and nodding ever so slightly.

They stood that way for a minute or so, till finally she blurted out, "My God, Hawk. Don't you know me? I'm your cousin, Cassy!"

11

Later, he would try to reconstruct that lunch at the Chinese restaurant and it would seem like a dream, as insubstantial as a strand of yolk in egg-drop soup. As he followed Cassandra through the brightly done-up dining room, all black lacquer and green ferns, the place seemed shrouded in fog.

He was surrounded by a miasma of confusing emotions. On the one hand, he felt a sense of relief at coming upon someone with a common history—and in Denver, of all places. The experience was liberating, as though he'd suddenly been freed of a knee brace. Part of him felt like he could run full speed.

But he also felt mired in a fetid mound of guilt and fear. His cousin? That wasn't quite the way he'd been thinking about this woman. Ever since that first glimpse of her, at the Wynkoop on Friday afternoon, the feelings he'd been harboring toward Cassandra were scarcely familial.

As they were seated at a back table and received their menus, Hawk half-heard the waiter's litany: "Hi, I'm Jason and I'll be your server. How are you folks today?" He found himself high-centered, spinning wheels inside his mind.

His companion was looking at him expectantly, with a smile.

"Cousin, eh?" he said. "Well, I do remember someone like you, a little girl. Maybe twelve at the time. I was in college."

"Yes you were, and a big deal, too. At least in the circles

I moved in. Do you remember how our parents knew one another? How they'd left Delaware, come out to Kansas so we kids could go to Haskell? There were scholarships for Nanticokes. We used to see each other at powwows and such. I'm not surprised if you don't remember much about me. We're something like eight years apart."

"But you say we're cousins?" he asked. "I don't remember that."

Cassy shrugged. "I remember our parents were related."

Hawk felt the fog began to lift. Distant cousins? A flicker of hope stirred in his loins.

By the time they'd downed a couple of beers along with a main course of something wrapped in lettuce leaves, Hawk had learned a good deal more of Cassy's story. It seemed she'd entered Haskell back when it was a junior college, same as he. She'd completed her two-year degree in 1988, just as Indian tribes were receiving land-into-trust acquisitions to put up casinos. Casino operators were scouring the campus, looking for bright, attractive Native Americans, and Cassy had signed up for an interview. In ten minutes' time, she was hired.

She'd stayed for four years before returning to Haskell as a marketing major. In the meantime, in 1992, the school had become a four-year institution.

"So, if they'd had a four-year program all along, would you have stayed?"

"I don't think so. I needed to get out on my own. In fact, when I left, I didn't think I'd ever go back to school." She looked off, out the window.

"But something happened."

She looked back at Hawk, with a rueful smile. "There was a guy, a relationship that came to a bad end. I guess you've heard all that before. But, there was more... Have you spent much time around the gaming industry?"

"Did a story on it once, in Oklahoma. Seemed a lot like selling drugs."

Suddenly her eyes were ice. "That's dead wrong," she hissed. "Don't tell me you're one of those damn knee-jerk liberals. Same crap you see in all those so-called exposés."

"So, gambling's a good thing. Good for the red man. Good for the spirit."

"I didn't say that," Cassy snapped. "But it isn't necessarily addictive. Haven't you ever heard the stats? Alcohol dependence in the U.S.: 13.8 percent of the population. Drug dependence: 6.2 percent. Major depression: 6.4 percent. And gambling? Do you know what percentage of Americans are addicted to that? Less than one percent: 0.8 percent, to be exact."

Hawk raised an eyebrow. "And now for all the benefits to society. I remember getting fed that. What was it? Three quarters of all the revenue goes to tribal coffers: schools, community centers, and the like."

"As a matter of fact, that's right. Only twenty-five percent goes to individuals," she snapped. Hawk decided he liked the looks of this woman when her nostrils flared.

"Well, there's an interesting statistic: one out of four," he noted, dryly. "Isn't that the same percentage of gambling jobs that go to Indians?"

She looked down for a moment, then turned to find Jason, the server. When she caught his eye, she signaled for more coffee and made a scribbling in the air: the check. When she turned back, she had a puzzled expression.

"Do you notice there's a kind of hum in here?'

Hawk looked at her quizzically.

"An undercurrent. It's not what anyone is saying. It's the energy of all the conversations. It seems kind of frenetic. It's..."

"The buzz," Hawk said. "That's what we call it. It's the sound of everyone together, talking at the same time, trying to be heard. Some say it's the key ingredient for a successful restaurant in Denver. People don't come just for the food. They want to be where something's happening. They come for the buzz."

She looked at him intently. "It's a lot like a casino," she said. "And you? Do you like it?"

Hawk said, "After a while, I can't think. It gets to me. There's something in me that needs darkness and silence. So, you promised to tell me everything I should know about the video phone. Are you ready? Let's get out of here."

Wally Arneson stood at the entrance to his wood-paneled employees' lounge, shaking his head. The last of his programmers had cleaned out his desk, signed off on his time sheet and headed south on the express elevator.

The room was a mess, as if a cyclone had crossed paths with a food fight. Indeed, he wondered if he'd done the right thing, ordering in the sandwiches and fresh, thick onion rings from the Manhattan Deli downstairs. There were splotches of grease where the onions had been hurled against the walls. Here and there, a picture was cracked from one of the big blue buttons.

The buttons were all over, and Wally sighed as he gathered them up. One for each of the programmers on his team. He doubted he'd ever see them again. Sadly, his thoughts went back to the luncheon. Where had he gone wrong?

He'd considered several ways he might present the message he'd received from Granger Rowe, the new Vice President for Advanced Technology. The message would be unnerving, however it was put; that much he'd known.

"We're going a new direction," Granger Rowe had announced. It had been a blanket statement, delivered not in a personal message but as a conference call—maybe that was the worst part of it. Wally knew that, with the latest technology in conference calling, a thousand people could be dialed up at once. And he suspected Rowe may have addressed that many managers at Telwest.

He shuddered as he remembered all the rhetoric. "Going a new direction." New motto: "Nothing Stays the Same." There were new rules to go with the new direction, and they'd been spelled out. As a manager, you were heading: (1) a profit center, or (2) a cost center.

If your shop was not turning a profit, you had two months to bring to market whatever product you'd been developing. You could keep your employees, but only that long. Thereafter, expenses were to be paid out of revenues generated. That included a long list of line items, and payroll topped the list.

Wally had begun his staff meeting by summarizing the call. Then he'd thought about asking if there were any questions. There was a chance they could do something with the video phone in these two months, he'd decided, and he was ready to give a pep talk.

But as his gaze traversed around the room, his eye alighted on the sack he'd brought back from the Wynkoop. "Available for Reassignment." He'd started passing out the buttons. "AFR"—he'd spoken of the practice as a generous gesture on the part of Telwest.

"You know, someone might be needed in another department," he'd said. "That is, if they know you're available for hire. I've seen it happen."

But Grant Holdredge was having none of it, and he was lead programmer. "AFR," he'd reflected when handed his blue button. He'd picked it up and turned it over, scrutinizing it for a moment. Then, "AFR, my ass!" And he'd flung the thing at a glass-covered photograph signed by one of the Broncos.

In an instant, the others had followed his lead, and Wally never had found time to take questions. First the buttons, then the onion rings came sailing from all directions. When Gladys, the Office Mom, showed up at the door with a basketful of saucer-size, chocolate chip cookies, Wally had motioned her away.

So the programmers were gone now, to a man. Evidently, the job market in information technology wasn't so bad. These people may have enjoyed the camaraderie of working for Wally, but they didn't need Telwest. Not when, everywhere outside the floundering ex-utility, their industry was booming.

Wally picked up the last of the paper plates, and switched off the light to the lounge. It was midafternoon and the sun was hovering over the mountains. He'd have to take on the programming that needed to be done, see what it would take to finalize the address book technology. There was no one to call on.

Of course, he hadn't done this kind of work for a decade. He thought about that as he sank down into his big Naugahyde desk chair and switched on his computer. He'd employed others to do the programming. That was the level he'd attained in his career, like the big number 4 on his badge. But he knew all the buzz words. "Object-oriented programming: OPP. Relational data base systems. Interactive..." Whatever. He'd seen it on resumes of people he'd hired.

As the sun began to sink behind the looming mountains, he hunched over the computer and peered into his screen.

The lights were on and the front door unlocked as Hawk and Cassy returned to the Hermitage after lunch. Teresa was back on the job at the front desk, leafing through a stack of invoices. It seemed her little boy was better and she'd found a sitter for the afternoon. Her coal black hair was sparkling and she had her makeup on, but Hawk could see dark circles under her eyes.

As Hawk introduced the two women, Cassy commented, "He's my cousin, you know." He thought he saw Teresa stifle a smile. She must have picked up on his deflated look.

"Todd's in," Teresa said, "and he left this for you." For the second time, she presented him with the twelve-month lease agreement. "He said to stop by."

Hawk gave a knock as he swung open the door to Todd's office, and he ushered Cassy inside. Looking up at an angle, his chin cradling a telephone receiver, Todd motioned them to a pair of huge, maroon, leather chairs. The chairs looked unfamiliar and must have been recent additions to an office that already rivaled the lobby of a mountain lodge.

He watched Cassy ogle the scene with a little girl's smile: the mounted heads of bison, elk, and moose; the Indian rugs on pine-paneled walls; the big-screen television with its silent run of multicolored images on the news channel. She seemed almost entranced.

But as she turned back toward Todd, Hawk saw her wince. She must have sensed that he'd been staring at her all the while. Todd looked away and sat up straight. He was concentrating on his call now, nodding vigorously. Why do people gesture during telephone calls? Hawk had always wondered.

"Yes, sir. You bet," Todd exclaimed. "Of course I'll accept. I'm honored that you've asked me." As he hung up the phone, he was beaming. He flashed a grin at Cassy and held out his hand. She ignored it.

Todd turned to Hawk, ebullient. "You've heard of the Peak Society."

Hawk shook his head.

"Well, it's an exclusive organization. Not in the sense that they meet; but there's a record of the membership, and it's an honor to be listed. Top hundred leaders in Denver, that's what they are. And you know what? They've asked me to be in it."

Hawk offered his congratulations and introduced Cassy. She warmed up a little at Todd's wide-eyed, ingenuous excitement. Now she smiled and extended her hand.

He told Todd about the internship and the Haskell connection. Everything but the cousin part. Todd beamed and nodded as he scrutinized her hair.

"Well, Cassy's done some research on the video phone, Todd, and we're going to talk about it some before she starts working for Wally. It's a two-month assignment, you know. That's how long Wally has to make this thing pay." He paused and glanced meaningfully at the lease agreement in his hand.

But Todd wasn't paying attention. He'd been drawn off to some scene on the TV: a protest march in Latin America. Tear gas flying, people fleeing. While his partner was preoccupied, Hawk dropped the unsigned lease on his desk.

He motioned to Cassy and they stepped to the door. "So, Todd, we'll see you later. Congrats on the Peak thing. We'll be meeting down the hall, about the video phone. If you should need me, we'll be..."

Suddenly, Todd snapped to attention. He spun in their direction, the protest march a memory. "That's what I wanted to talk to you about. It was something you said a minute ago. The video phone. So, who's done the research?"

"It's Cassy, here. For her internship with Wally."

"Sure, of course. I remember." He gave a bashful grin. "That call came and I got distracted. Well, why don't the two of you sit down?"

Hawk was amazed at Cassy's poise, as she reached into her briefcase and pulled out some notes on her research. She seemed to have so many sides to her personality. That had been clear the first few hours they'd been together. One moment, she was lost in wonder at the sight of Todd's office. Then a glint of anger, at his stare. In an instant, she was friendly again, in tune with his excitement over the Peak Society. Now she was all business. She was no ordinary college girl, but a young woman who'd spent four years in the grit and glitter of the gambling industry and kept her soul intact.

He noticed that she gave a kind of sign as she shifted gears. She'd nod and blink, more or less signaling that some new side of her was in the wings. Now she took out a note card and looked up with a smile.

"The video phone," she began. "It's not a new product. Sixty years in development. First introduced to the public at the World's Fair of 1960."

Hawk said, "Yeah, so the question is: why hasn't it caught on?"

"Do you always have to be so negative?" Todd snapped.

Cassy also turned to him and glared. He couldn't be sure, in her case, but he thought it might have been mock anger.

"From the perspective of history, the video phone makes all the sense in the world, don't you think?" she continued, rhetorically. "I mean, first there were photographs, then moving pictures. First there was radio, and now..." She motioned toward the television. "So, when people have the ability to talk to someone on the phone, why wouldn't they want to see the person on the other end of the line, as well?"

Hawk thought about Teresa's offhand comment, that morning when she'd called to say she was staying home: "I'm glad you can't see me," she'd said. He was considering whether to risk another negative observation, when Todd blurted out, "Well, sometimes we don't look so hot. Like when I'm hunting. It's a good time to be off-camera."

Cassy smiled. "Well, there's the option of turning off the video. That's always been a feature of the video phone. But what's the other problem? Why hasn't a technology like this caught on?"

"Could be the cost," Hawk surmised. "How much would you have to put out for one of these things? A couple of thou? And, besides that, what good is it going to do you if you call somebody up and they don't have one?"

"That's true," Todd admitted. "It'd be like broadcasting over television if no one had a set."

"So, what happened with television?" Cassy asked, rhetorically. "Wasn't there a time when sets were expensive and there were very few programs? And then, as more people bought them, more were made, and the price went down."

"Economies of scale," Hawk noted. "Sure, that happens. But why not with the video phone?"

"There are theories," said Cassy, and she shuffled her cards. "One is that you need a group of people who'll commit to it, demonstrate what it can do."

"That's it!" Todd suddenly sat bolt upright. "The P-Peak Society." he sputtered. "They can't get people to come to meetings, but they need to be in contact. Hey, it's a slam dunk. Those guys'd be hot for video phone!

"Say, I'm glad Hawk found you. First productive thing he's done in a month. You want an office? Hawk, there's that extra room down your way, you know." Todd swung round in his desk chair, reaching for his Rolodex. "I'm going to call some of my buddies down at the station. Live at Five! News you can use. The video phone. What a concept!"

Cassy winced. "Well, okay," she said. "But there's one other..."

Hawk caught her eye and shook his head. He motioned toward the door.

Down the hall, they opened the door to a small office next to his own. He turned on the light and pulled up the blinds. "Think you could live with this?"

Cassy set down her briefcase and looked around. She

took a seat in her desk chair and swiveled it full circle. When she came back 'round, she looked up and smiled. "The place could use a plant or two, but I think I'd like it fine—right here next door to my cousin."

Hawk grimaced and she gave a grin. "Say, can I tell you the other point I had in mind?"

Hawk leaned against the door jamb.

"You see, a new technology has to fill some obvious purpose," she said. "It has to meet a need, to show there is something it can do far better than anything else on the market, and that the thing it can do is important."

"Um, I think I know what you're talking about," Hawk responded. "What do they call it? 'The killer application.' It's like the spreadsheet made the market for the personal computer. Before they came up with that way to use it, nobody would buy one."

"That's it," she said. "'The killer app.' The compelling application."

"And how long does it take to come up with something like that?" Hawk thought about Wally and his AFR badge. Two months' reprieve, for all of them.

"So, what's the 'killer app' for the video phone, Cassy? It's got to be more than this Peak Society stuff. Any inspiration?"

"I'm afraid not," she admitted. "But there is one hopeful sign."

"And what's that?'

"Wally says he has one."

As Cassy turned to arranging her desk, Hawk headed down the hall to Todd's office. "The killer app." Perhaps he could cram one more concept into his partner's cranium. But he stopped just outside the door.

Todd was back on the phone. "Well, I'm glad you like it. The Peak Society, the video phone. Hey, once in a while even I can come up with... Like I said, Vern, I thought we might run it by the TV guys, see if anybody...

"You mean there's more to the story? Yeah, I understand. Not for publication... Sure, I've heard of caller ID. Been around for a few years...

"I know. We think it's just for home phones. But businesses, too. People calling in for pizza, or whatever. So you guys can keep track..."

"But how do you think we could sell it?"

Hawk winced and shook his head. He turned back toward his office.

12

Next morning, the Hermitage was humming. Teresa came in early, dressed to the nines. There was an ambitious air about her, as though she was glad to be at work again. Cassy had bought a couple of plants and was fixing up her office. Hawk saw that Todd had shut his door. After the phone conversation he'd overheard, he wondered what was going on in there.

Teresa told him that Todd had been working intently on a flyer to be faxed to the members of the Peak Society. About ten o'clock, he came by and tossed a copy on Hawk's desk.

THE NEXT BIG THING

Telwest presents the leading edge of telecommunications technology:

THE VIDEO PHONE

Haven't you always wished you could check out the person you're talking to?

Now you can, with the video phone.

A special offer to the Peak Society.

Try it, with no cost or obligation.

The flyer closed with the phone number and name of their firm, Mountain High Communications. It said someone named "Cassy" would be calling shortly.

"So, what do you think, *amigo?*"

As Hawk perused the flyer, he found himself pondering his thoughts about Todd. Since yesterday, the clouds that had enshrouded the two of them had cracked open to a few rays of sunshine. Meeting with Cassy, they'd begun to behave again as partners, tossing around ideas instead of jousting over disagreements. Still, there was the matter of the lease. That hadn't changed.

Hawk looked up to see if Todd had brought it along. Thank God! He was empty-handed.

"Well, Todd, it has some juice; it's arresting. But when were you planning to send it out?"

"This morning."

Hawk paused. "Why don't you fax it over to Wally? I'll call him. We need to be sure the video phone actually works, for one thing. I mean, I've never seen one in operation. Have you?"

Todd shook his head.

"Plus, somebody better confirm that Telwest wants their name on it."

Todd looked down with a frown.

"And there's one other thing," Hawk added. "Why don't you go next door and show it to Cassy?"

Todd took off and Hawk savored the quiet space to think a moment. So, how did a company like Telwest make decisions? Much quicker than before, he knew that much. He'd heard these corporations were shaped more like diamonds than pyramids—lots of decision-makers in the middle rather than just a few at the top. Faster turnaround, more autonomy. But still they had to have some procedure for processing a new product, testing it out.

And there must be somebody competent at the top. Someone like Granger Rowe.

Two minutes later, Todd was back. He stumbled into Hawk's office and closed the door behind him. "Houston, we have a problem," he announced.

Hawk looked up, expecting the lease.

"She wants to be called 'Cassandra.'"

Hawk breathed a sigh of relief. "Well, from what I heard, that's her given name: Cassandra Harmon."

"But I heard you call her 'Cassy.'"

"That's because I'm a kind of relative. And a friend, maybe. Anyway, I think people should be called whatever makes them feel comfortable."

"Well, I don't feel comfortable." Todd sat down, with a worried glance Hawk's way. "And maybe that brings up something else we need to talk about."

Hawk set down his pen, ready for the twelve-month confrontation.

"Well, I don't know how to put this, exactly. But... what is she?"

Hawk sat a moment. "I'm not sure what you mean. She's a young woman, age twenty-four. She's our marketing intern, a student at Haskell All Nations University."

"I don't mean all of that, and you know it," Todd said with a wary grin. "Hey, you know, Hawk. Ethnic stuff. What kind of race is she?"

Hawk pushed back from his desk and stood, slowly. He stepped to the window for a moment before he turned around. He paused, to get control of himself before the flames that smoldered inside rose higher. He walked back toward Todd and stood there staring down. As Todd peered up at his looming partner, there was a flickering tic at his left eyelid, and his grin began to wrench into a grimace.

Just then, they heard a knock at the door. Hawk opened it and it was Cassy. "I'm going over to meet with Wally. Anything you have for him?"

Hawk picked up the flyer and jotted some notes on it before handing it back to her. As she walked out, she flashed a warm smile in his direction. She glanced down at Todd with a puzzled frown.

Cassy heard the elevator "ping" as it approached the thirty-second floor. Although there were eighteen floors above it, no one else was riding on the elevator. She remembered that the building had been more crowded when she'd met with Wally the week before. Had Telwest lost that many jobs?

As the elevator came to a stop, the door slid open and she looked up with a start. Everything was in darkness. Had she punched the wrong floor? No, this was thirty-two. But she could still envision the scene the week before: lights shining, computers whirring in the cubicles. She recalled at least a dozen scruffy programmers. Plus that strange lady hauling a red wagon with all the junk food.

Cassy stepped out of the elevator and looked deep into the shadows cast by the dim light that came creeping through the blinds. It was hard to imagine that it was 10:30 in the morning. But she could see well in the darkness. In fact, if the truth were known, she often preferred it to the light. Sometimes the world looked clearer at dusk than in daylight.

She thought of Hawk's comment about needing darkness and silence.

Then she remembered why she was here. It had everything to do with seeing things for what they were, with objectivity. With all the reasons she had turned her back on the gossamer world of the gambling industry. Plying retirees with free, watered drinks, suggesting they amounted to something. Selling them hope, one hand in their pocket, in a casino clouded with smoke and dark mirrors.

None of that now. Marketing was a science. Either there was a demand for this video phone contraption or there wasn't. It was her job to find out ...

And, yet, there was this other side to things. For a moment, she gave herself over to the silence and the shadows. She put off ringing for the elevator to go back down, and simply stood there.

It was then she saw the light shining through a crack in the door, far across the abandoned floor. It was coming from the corner where Wally had his office. She started toward it through a maze of cracker box cubicles.

Cassy knocked and then swung the door open. The office was empty, but it was evident that someone had been working there. On one wall, a white board was covered with scribbled notations. A diagram of something. At the top, it read: PEEK SOCIETY. She grinned; these geeks never could spell. Below that: Address Book. Then: Key Field, and Links. She vaguely recalled a course in computers. What was all that: components of a database management system?

On a table in the middle of the room were half a dozen manuals, pages marked by Post-its. There was an ash tray spilling over and a couple of half-filled coffee cups. It seemed Wally had pulled an all-nighter. Should she wait here? Perhaps he was coming back. Or, she could just leave a note.

Cassy scavenged his desk for a note pad, and that's when she noticed an odd device at one corner of it. It looked like a cross between a telephone and a computer. There was a phone receiver at the base and, above that, a monitor. Of course—a video phone. Well, it's about time she'd seen one.

She found a pad, and got as far as, "Wally, I came by," when a kind of clicking erupted from the video phone. An incoming call? Then the clicks turned into a whirring sound. After a couple of seconds, the screen went blue as the phone began to ring. Three rings, then four. Should she answer? But a recording came on, in a halting voice. "Uh, this is Wally Arneson. Leave a message and I'll get back..." Then a beep, as the blue screen turned to flesh tones.

"Hello, Wally," said the woman on the screen. "How's the reception?"

Cassy recognized the middle-aged woman seated at the edge of a bed. She'd seen her in the office last week, with the red wagon. But now she was wearing nothing but her underwear. Smiling coyly, the woman reached behind her back and unhooked her brassiere. She dropped the bra, and presented two massive breasts to the camera. Then she stood up and slowly drew off her panties.

Cassy felt her breath catch in her throat. She felt like an intruder, yet she was fascinated. The woman on the video phone drew down the bed clothes. She lowered herself onto the bed and, with the same, wan smile, she slid her fingers down and began rubbing. The phone beeped again, as the screen returned to blue. At the end, she was moaning. "Wally, call me."

13

"So, I have a question. And I hope it's not indiscreet."

They were sitting at the Starbucks the next day and, halfway through a swallow of coffee, Hawk broke into a fit of coughing.

"God, I hope not, Cassy," he sputtered as she passed him a glass of water. He was well aware of a indiscretion or two he might have in mind.

Finally, he said, "I thought we were just coming here to celebrate your first sales call for the video phone."

"We are," she assured him with a smile. "And thanks for hiking over. I needed a damn break." She surveyed the Starbucks from the back booth they'd found. "You know, late in the morning it's not so crowded in here."

"So, how did it go?" Hawk asked.

"I'll tell you what. That Vern Warner—you know, the CIO? He was all over this video phone."

"Like hair on a gorilla," Hawk cracked. "Like maggots on carrion..."

"Pretty much," she went on, ignoring him. "He wanted to be sure he was the first member of the Peak Society to sign up for the thing, and he knew quite a bit about it. It almost seemed like he'd had a briefing before I got there."

"I have no doubt he had," Hawk said. He told her about the phone call he'd overheard outside Todd's office.

"Which brings me back to my question." She stopped and took a long draught of coffee, before looking up at him.

"Hawk, how much do you know about what we're doing? You see, the other day, when I was in Wally's office..."

By the end of her story, Hawk thought he saw her skin grow darker. Was she blushing? Gladys, the Office Mom, had been "fooling with herself," she said.

When she finished, Hawk simply smiled and shrugged. "How much do I know?" he asked. "How much do I need to know? That's the operative question. It's how I've stayed in business with Todd for the past four years."

"But I thought you guys were partners."

He nodded with a rueful smile. "We are, in the sense that we share an office suite. We're each responsible for half of the expenses." Hawk shuddered. He'd been trying not to think about the lease.

"But, beyond meeting expenses, Todd goes his way and I go mine. Or, at least I could if..."

"If you were to get any new clients," Cassy added.

He looked down, silent. "I see you've been talking to Teresa."

She smirked then she sat in silence.

"Well, Cassy, I guess the short form of the story is that Todd takes on all kinds of business, and it's no affair of mine. I don't know half of what he gets into, and I don't care to. I'm sure he doesn't understand half of it himself.

"And, speaking of the man of the hour, I need to watch the time. We're supposed to meet for lunch at noon."

When he turned back to Cassy, she was studying him closely. "But this is different, isn't it? This video phone thing. Don't you have to understand this? Doesn't it seem like we're all in this together?"

Casa de Manuel was the kind of place you went for lunch if you didn't care who saw you. The café sat hunkered down on the 2200 block of Larimer Street, within walking distance of the new ball park and the renovated, red brick warehouses of lower downtown that were drawing high-tech firms like horse flies to a stable. On one side of Manuel's was an upscale fern bar that featured quiche and wines from the Sonora Valley. On the other side, a pawn shop where vagrants might be found collapsed on the sidewalk or urinating against a wall.

Inside Manuel's were the best chili rellenos and smothered bean burritos in downtown Denver, at prices that would put fast-food outlets to shame. Hawk turned back his menu when the waitress came by with chips and salsa, and she simply nodded. The usual: a bean burrito smothered in green chili, a barbacoa taco, and a beef tamale. Todd ordered one of the combination plates, ready-made for the patrons who didn't know to choose from the side orders.

Todd dipped a chip in the red sauce and raised it as a toast. "So, how long has it been since we had lunch together?"

Hawk shook his head. "Long enough to let some things build up, I guess. It feels like we have a few things to work out. Let's talk a little about Cassy."

He knew he had a few minutes of his partner's attention, before the food arrived, and so he took him through a cram course in American racial history.

How many racial groups are there in the United States? Todd said maybe three: black, white, and Hispanic. Hawk said it was more like 200.

He talked about the "colored" people who predated the Civil War: groups such as the Creoles and Cajuns. Neither white nor black, but "free people of color." The Melungeons in the back woods of Appalachia, thought to have been descended from Portuguese sailors shipwrecked off the coast of Virginia.

And the Nanticoke.

As the steaming plates of entrees arrived at the table,

Hawk launched into the story of a tribe first sighted in 1608 by the English colonist Captain John Smith of Jamestown and Pocahontas fame. The Nanticoke looked a bit different from other Indians to the English. They were darker. And they behaved differently—a hostile bunch who shot arrows at the colonizers instead of welcoming them as had the other Indians.

The Nanticoke were a proud tribe, Hawk said. They called themselves "People from the Rising Sun." But, in time, they were defeated by the colonizers. Some of them fled to Canada, where the purebred version could still be found. Those who stayed in America interbred with blacks and whites, which helped them survive a lot of the diseases brought by Europeans. But, as a tribe, they were thought to have vanished, hybridized out of existence.

"Then, one day in 1856," Hawk went on, "a shop owner in Delaware was arrested. Levin Sockum was accused of selling ammunition to his son-in-law, Isaac Harmon. Same surname as Cassandra. Seems, in Delaware, it was illegal to possess firearms if you were black."

"Okay," Todd said, " that's unfair. But, cut to the chase. What does that have to do with the Nanticokes?"

"Have another tortilla. You see, these guys were viewed as blacks. But when they came to trial, Sockum stood up and announced they weren't Negro at all. They were Nanticoke, Native Americans. And they went out and found a member of the tribe, an old lady who still spoke the language, to back up their claim. The defense worked; they were acquitted. After that trial, other Nanticokes were found. Within twenty-five years they became a legal tribe, 'a special class of colored people.'"

"And that's what you are? Is that what you're telling me?" Todd asked.

"Cassy, as well," Hawk told him.

"Seems complicated as hell," Todd said. "Wouldn't it be

easier just to call yourselves 'black?' I mean, they're made up of all different races anyhow."

Hawk looked away and thought a minute.

"There have been times I've been tempted to try. But, it's not that simple. There are differences, even with Nanticokes who look black. We don't behave like African Americans. We're not much into music, for one thing. Or formal religion. We're quiet, spiritual in a different sort of way. And one other thing."

Hawk smiled as he thought of first meeting Cassy. "We walk single file."

On the way back to the office, Todd fell in line behind him and, for the first time in memory, the two of them laughed. They walked a block in silence.

"So, what do you want to do about the lease?" Hawk asked.

Todd stopped and turned to his partner. He wasn't smiling. He pulled a sheet of paper out of his jacket pocket and handed it to Hawk. "I was going to give it to you back at the office," he said. "My lawyer drew it up."

Hawk glanced at the document and grasped it at once. The agreement put Todd in charge of promoting the video phone, though both of them would bear legal responsibility for the venture and they would divide any profits. Hawk was to play a liaison role, both with Wally and in supervising Cassandra. Todd would make all of the promotional decisions. There'd be no more vacillating over what to do. In return, Todd would take full responsibility for the twelve-month lease.

He looked up. Todd was holding a pen. Hawk went over the document once more. He slowly took the pen. He knew he had no choice but to sign it.

14

Granger Rowe straddled his sleek, black chair like a classic Harley as he scooted back and forth along his desktop. His chair glistened in the morning sun, like the pomade on his sable hair. The desk ran the full length of a floor-to-ceiling window that framed the Rocky Mountains for him, and Rowe reveled in it.

His chair may not have been as big as some—there were, after all, restrictions on the size of office furniture for vice presidents at Telwest—but it was mobile. In the throes of a conference call on his speaker phone, Granger could snag a memo from a stack of correspondence at the south end of his twenty-foot desk and re-file it on the northern extremity in a matter of seconds.

Today, however, he was not in conference. As usual, he was spending his morning studying telecommunications terminology. It was a good time to mull over this strange, arcane material, before the sun passed over his office building and bored straight through his window. By two o'clock, it was time to draw the blinds, before the heat became unbearable. The afternoon sun was one of the topics they hadn't covered when he was hired out of the hotel industry.

Granger was working through piles of acronyms, and he had them all on flash cards. ISDN and DSL: two methods of transmitting data at high speed over phone lines. CUI and GUI: even stranger-sounding acronyms. He tried to spell out the words as he sped back and forth. The other executives batted them around like small talk at a cocktail party, and before long they'd expect him to catch on. From CUI to GUI: what was that about? He picked up two cards at the Wyoming end of his desktop and went careening down to place them in his to-do pile. Oh, sure: from "character user interface" to "graphical user interface."

Whatever the hell that meant.

Granger reached for another stack of flash cards. But just then there was a knock on the door and Allison stepped in from the outer office. Granger put down his cards, glad for the diversion. She was a willowy young woman with auburn hair who dressed like a resort ad: an endless array of designer jeans and svelte sweaters. Allison never failed to capture Granger's attention, even though for ten years he had seen her almost every day. She'd been his trusted assistant at the Summit Group, the hotel chain where he'd worked before, and it had been a condition of his contract that she come with him to Telwest.

Allison sorted through his correspondence several times a day, deciding which subjects ought to occupy his attention. As she entered, she passed by a photograph of Granger's family at the south end of his desk, then walked over to inspect his computer monitor. She paused at the image on the screen and smiled. The screensaver was her photo.

Today, she brought in a sheet fresh off the fax machine and handed it to Granger, with a pinch on the back of his neck. He turned and winked, for a moment off the fast track. He saw that the fax was from Vern Warner, the CIO at Telwest. Hadn't he just met him at the strategic planning confab the other day? The guy appeared a little old for the job, but he had some good traits—seemed like kind of a conniver.

He scanned the fax, and his eyes went wide the instant he took in the heading: THE NEXT BIG THING. Oh, wow! Now they were talking.

He read on about the video phone, and it was exciting.

What a concept. Granger munched mouthfuls of popcorn as he thought about the flyer, surging to and fro in his turbo chair. He ate popcorn without butter or salt, in a losing effort to keep his weight down, along with his blood pressure. Most days, he changed into oversized sweat shirts and loose-fitting jeans so he could work out impromptu on the Nautilus machine at the far end of his office. But, whatever his rigors, at age forty-something, Granger Rowe had the body of a half-inflated football.

Granger handed the flyer back to Allison with a thumbs up. She should call and accept the offer: video phones for members of the Peak Society. He remembered the Society. Last week, he'd been asked to join. An organization that never met—for people too busy to attend meetings. What a concept.

Granger loved innovations like the Peak Society and the video phone—and Denver was full of them. What he didn't like was the details of technology. All these fucking flash cards.

As he watched Allison all the way out the door, he thought about the flyer again. Hadn't it said "Telwest?" That must mean one of his technical people was involved. He wrote himself a note in his Daytimer. Find out who's heading up the video phone department.

Granger Rowe had a number of core skills as a corporate manager. One of them was benchmarking: transferring best practices from one industry to another. For Granger, an industry was nothing but a "space"—an environment where creative guys could test out new ideas. A clever guy could flit back and forth among industries the way athletes could sign contracts with new teams.

As an exec in the hospitality field, hospitals had come by to ask him how a typical hotel could register a guest in less than five minutes, while their patients waited two hours to be attended by a doctor. That was the idea behind benchmarking, to think outside the box. It was why Telwest had recruited a technology manager from outside the telecom field.

But Granger had another specialty, and that was downsizing. Or, as he liked to think of it, "rightsizing." He knew how to set up systems for evaluating employees and "uninstalling" the ones who weren't needed. It was a skill he knew he could market in almost any field.

In the afternoons, just after lunch, he turned his attention to a huge chart that took up most of his east wall. It was a colorful chart, made up of a thousand names on panels of red and blue and yellow. The chart was like a living mosaic of constantly shifting colors. And for technology managers at Telwest, the patterns had a life-and-death significance.

If the panel behind a person's name was blue, the color of the corporate logo, his position was secure. Yellow was for caution, like the traffic light. And red? Well, those were the guys who got two months' notice.

Now he turned to his computer and switched on a database of all the managers who reported to him. He'd sent a message to the lot of them in his mass conference call, asked them to send him proposals for continuing their operations. It was a simple procedure: zero-based budgeting. The ones who couldn't come up with a convincing argument would be out in the cold.

Granger bounced in his chair as the program booted up. This was the most difficult part of his day, at the computer screen, for Granger couldn't bear to sit still. Allison had made up a file of all the proposals that had come in. He knew a lot of them would be technical—dull, boring shit—and he'd have to look up half the words. How many were there today? Oh, God: a dozen new ones.

He clicked on the first proposal. Well, hey! It was about the video phone, from some guy named WallyArneson. So he's the one in charge of that operation. He looked up his name on the chart. The guy was shaded red. Two months' notice, dead meat. But he remembered the flyer and turned to the text. Shit. It was typical engineer-speak. Next steps in programming, and all that. He scanned to the new product features. A video messaging system, now in place. Next feature: an address book for the video phone.

Warner, the CIO, had added a note on another new wrinkle: caller ID. Someone calls in for a product or service, these days you could keep track of who was calling.

But what was the point? You sure as hell couldn't sell enough of these gizmos to outfits like the Peak Society. Where's the market? Granger scrolled to the next section of the proposal and, as he began reading, he settled down and stopped squirming.

He buzzed for Allison and she came back in. She pulled up a chair and they read together. It was interesting, the research on telecommunications and human behavior. He liked to have Allison in on this part of the work. She'd been a psych major at Vassar, honors grad. Sometimes she got excited, and her face flushed. He liked her like that. But often she was more restrained, and he knew he needed that from her as well.

According to Arneson's sources, the average phone call transmits thirty percent less energy than a face-to-face conversation. Almost a third less. Could be an argument for the video phone. But, where was that important? Why did that matter? They took a moment and put their heads together.

Somewhere, they'd seen a list of growth sectors in the communications industry. Allison got up to look in her files. And there it was—a sector that had been growing twice as fast as all the rest, throughout the 1990s. It seemed record numbers of Americans had been dialing up on 900 numbers—the kind of call where the consumer picks up the tab—and why were they calling? His eyes went wide when he identified the product.

Whoa! Talk about a growth industry. Those dudes weren't ordering pizza.

Allison gave a quizzical smile as they got to the end of the marketing piece. She was squinting, mulling over the data, while Granger was rollicking with laughter. Talk about a killer app! He leapt from his chair and twirled Allison around in hers. Then he scooted over to his multicolored wall chart. He ran his finger down the column till he found the name he was looking for. With the flick of a switch, Wally Arneson took a step back from the cliff. Granger transformed him from a bright red to a yellow.

Hawk popped the tab on a cold can of guava juice and settled back in a wicker chair at Friendly's Abs Lab. His body felt relaxed after an hour's workout before lunch time. And yet, he found himself nervously scanning the snack bar. The décor was nothing special, all mauve and gray, like half the eateries in Denver. The interior decorators who put up this vapid stuff must work to the accompaniment of New Age music, he was thinking. Why was he staring at it?

Then he realized why he was uneasy. He was trying to avoid gazing at an apparition with golden-bronze skin and flowing black hair, in a warm-up suit of perfectly blended turquoise and sand. His cousin sat across the table, and it was hard to keep his eyes off her. "His cousin"—damn! Would he ever get past that? More important, would she? Had she? Now he noticed her quizzical expression.

"Wazzup, Hawk?"

"Just thinking."

"Well, maybe you can do that for both of us. I need to relax, away from that office. What a madhouse. I tell you, if we didn't come over here every day, I don't know what I'd do. By the way, it's my turn to buy lunch."

"No need, Cassy. You're an intern, remember?"

"That's what I'd thought. Right now, I feel more like

a receptionist. All those damn phone messages. None of these Peak Society guys are ever in."

"They're busy boys," he enjoined. "You've just got to stay with it. Reminds me of what some old guy in PR once told me. 'Public relations is just your basic blocking and tackling. But somebody's gotta do it.'"

There was a long pause. "Bullshit!"

Hawk looked up with a start. He hadn't been watching her countenance for a change in the weather. "How's that?" he asked.

"Ease up on the rhetoric, Hawk. I get enough of it from your partner, manic Todd. Problem is, he believes crap like that. I didn't think you did."

As she turned away, Hawk thought he saw a tear at the corner of her eye.

"C'mon, Cassy. Let's go get some lunch and we'll talk about it some. You don't need to get right back. Remember, you're working for me."

When Allison came back an hour later, she found Granger hunched over his desk with a stack of documents a half-foot high. He sat stock still, for once, absorbed in his task. The afternoon sun was boring through the window, but he didn't seem to notice.

She stood at the door and watched him. For the most part, she had a sense she understood him. The hunger for attention. The compulsion to compete, and the simple, greedy confidence he'd win. She'd known guys like this in college. Ivy Leaguers, most of them, with doting fathers who'd convinced them they could do no wrong. Granger was like that, if lagging a bit in the IQ League. That was where she came in.

Most times, she believed, she could get inside his head. And other times, she thought it didn't matter. Years ago, as a kid on her bike, she'd had a flash of insight. She'd imagined the world as a kind of road race. There were men and there were women, on the same course. But the fellows were in sports cars, the girls on bicycles.

She'd thought about the message she'd been handed: train hard, and you could be the fastest cyclist. But suddenly she saw through it. Sooner or later, if you had any sense, you put the bike aside. You spruced up and stood by the side of the road, vying for a ride in the fastest roadster.

Were there hazards on the road? No doubt.

Granger seemed to be in a race without a finish line. He'd already worked in three or four different industries, consuming them in the course of a few years. Wolfing them down like his popcorn. Tiring of them.

Where would that leave her, a few years down the road? Who knew? But 'til now, she'd had no complaints. Granger's career had been a great ride. As long as he kept on winning.

She stepped closer and saw what he was working on, a stack of marketing studies on the phone sex industry. At the thought of the video phone, she broke into a sly grin. Talk about adding value! But in an instant, she remembered what she was there for and the laughter inside her faded. She walked up to Granger and put her arm around his shoulder, the way she did when she brought sobering news.

Together, they looked at the front-page headline in the *Chronicle*:

THIRD QUARTER EARNINGS PLUMMET AT TELWEST
INVESTORS THREATEN LAWSUIT

Granger flinched for a second, then wheeled around in his chair. He motioned to the marketing studies, pumped his fist. Then he swung over to the calendar. With a week left in September, there was still time to put a spin on it, send a message to investors. *Voilà*—the video phone!

But there was more. Allison had brought along a flowchart with the names of a half-dozen Telwest workers and their job functions. At the top, it read: QUALITY ASSURANCE TEAM, PRODUCT DEVELOPMENT. It seemed there was indeed a procedure for checking things out.

Granger cringed; he hated delays, and the headlines in the *Chronicle* made him antsy. But he followed Allison all the way over to the multicolored wall chart. They began calling up the members of the Quality Assurance Team. But, one after another, they failed to appear. They tried it once more with the same result, then sat for a time and stared at the chart.

It seemed the QA group was history. In the latest wave of downsizing, the members had been let go, every one.

She'd asked where he lived as they left the Abs Lab with their gym bags, and he thought he'd test the waters. They picked up ribs to take out and grabbed a cab. He'd walked in to the office and they could take his car back after lunch. Now they were out on his seventh floor patio, enjoying the warmth of the late afternoon sun and overlooking the wooded terrain of Cheesman Park.

"So that's why I paired up with Todd, in spite of our differences," he was saying. "It was time to get away from the newsroom. And I wanted to try living in style for a while. I'd had enough of counting my nickels as a newspaper reporter."

She was silent for a while. They listened to the breeze in the trees, and felt the warm sun of an Indian summer. Finally, she spoke up.

"And what'll you do if this doesn't work out?" she asked. "This video phone gig. What do we have here, two months?"

"In answer to your first question, I have no clue. I think there might be a spot for me back at the *Chronicle*, depending on what they'd want me to do. I'd sure as hell never go back to what I was."

She looked at him inquiringly: "And what was that?"

He found he couldn't say the words, so he started to tell her the story. He set out to think of the managing editor's name, and couldn't. Then he tried again, but came up short.

Well, what did it matter? Just a name, and a man, to be forgotten. All he could remember was his demeanor. Some middle-aged white guy who'd been transferred out of Denver to another of the papers owned by a media conglomerate based in the Midwest. It was common. Being transferred around the country was what happened to white guys in their forties. At a certain stage of their working lives, it was what they did.

"So, you were what?" Cassy asked again. And Hawk became aware that once again he'd stopped talking. He was staring at the last glowing light at the tops of the trees.

The editor had been famous for his smile, and that was notable in the newspaper game. It was a profession where diffident reporters who wrote well could wake up one day to find themselves way out of their depth, thrown into the maelstrom of management. There was a saying in the trade: "A journalist is an introvert with a license to be an asshole."

But this guy was an exception. He knew how to work with people, and he had this smile. He was a polished, professional manager.

Hawk remembered how the editor had greeted him when he went in for his interview, the same day he was hired. He thought of the glittering smile. Then he noticed Cassy, looking at him quizically. He had to go on.

He tried to share a fleeting impression. It was the way he'd seen the editor eyeing him, squinting, behind the smile. Later, when he'd left the paper, he castigated himself. He should have been alert to the underside of that editor, as the guy was offering him a job as a GA, a general assignment reporter. It was a fine starting place for a fresh graduate. A good break—jobs in journalism were hard to come by. And on a major daily! He'd felt a rush of energy, and a surge of confidence in a future he could already envision unfolding. Thank God he'd gone to Kansas University, one of the best journalism programs in the country.

He ought to have suspected there was more to it than that.

Two years down the road, he'd come in one morning to find the message slip on his desk. A note to call the editor's secretary for an appointment. That was when he might have suspected what the fellow had in mind. This time, the smile was even broader. For Hawk had been promoted to beat reporter. It was a big step up from GA, with an equivalent increase in salary.

Once again, Hawk had felt warm all over as he laid back and basked in his editor's praise. My, how well he'd performed as a general assignment reporter! What a great job, digging out all those stories. Well, perhaps that was no surprise. It seemed that the editor himself was a KU grad.

"And what beat will I cover?" Hawk had finally thought to ask.

The man perused some notes on his desk, then turned to Hawk with an expectant smile. But this time he'd picked up that hint of a squint beneath it.

"Why, minority affairs. That's what it says right here," the editor had said. And, with that, he'd got up and proffered his hand. He ushered Hawk out to his new desk in another section of the newsroom. The interview was done.

"Jesus, Hawk, they hurt you," Cassy was saying when, bit by bit, he'd blurted out the story. "I could see that in your eyes as you were telling me."

He took a deep breath. "Well, there was more. One day, they slapped a black power button on me. Plastered some pomade on my hair to kink up the curls. Sent me out to cover a civil rights march. And the next day, it was a powwow. I got a lapel pin with a feather."

He remembered how the rage had washed over him. He stopped again. All he said was, "About then I ran into Todd and we started talking."

Cassy shook her head and made a gagging sound. Then she was silent.

"But, hey, Chief, you still owe me an answer to the second question. Do you think we can pull this off in two months?"

Hawk looked off across the trees and gave a sad chuckle. "I have no idea. But I do know one thing. Just then, you didn't call me 'cousin.'" He looked into her eyes and held out his hand.

As she took his hand, Cassy drew him to his feet and pulled him close, her head against his chest. They stood that way for a long time in the warm, autumn sunlight till their eyes met again, and they turned and walked inside.

15

By midafternoon there was talk of dinner. The office was a lost cause. Hawk phoned in and asked Teresa to give Todd a message. Something about conferring with Cassy on strategic planning. He thought he heard her snicker.

Soon they were back in their warm-up suits, in the living room with cans of Coors Light. Hawk dug up a sweater for Cassy, a big blue one with KU in red letters on the front, and they laughed at how it fit her like a tent. They sat on the couch and looked out over the treetops at the gathering dusk.

"You can see a lot from up here," Cassy murmured.

Hawk thought about that. He said, "You can see a lot in the shadows."

Cassy sat bolt upright and looked at him, sharply. "I thought I was the only one who felt that way."

Hawk said, "I hate to bring up our ancestors, or you'll start doing your cousin-thing. But, you know, that's why I believe the English settlers thought our guys were necromancers."

"Thought they were what?"

"Conjurers. Seers. They thought our ancestors were into magic. It was a natural assumption. You see, to the English, these Nanticokes suddenly appeared out of the forest. But in fact they'd been back there a long time—watching from the shadows. You can see better from back in there, rather than out in the sunlight. So they understood a lot of things about the settlers that the English couldn't see in themselves. Hell, you can always see better from the shadows."

"Works for me. And what do you see for the video phone, Chief? Hey, remember that second question?" She gave his thigh a nudge with her knee.

"I'm not sure," Hawk acknowledged. "I'd like to know what Wally has in mind. And, what's got into Todd? It seems like more than the Peak Society. I get a sense there's something going on in town. Something's building."

Just then, Cassy's stomach gave a low moan. She laughed and slugged Hawk on the shoulder, "Can you guess what else is building?"

Hawk got up and fished out a pizza menu from a pile on his desk. They were pleased to find they could agree on sausage and onion. He placed the call.

When he hung up the phone, he looked puzzled. "You know, I haven't ordered pizza for a while. But that was weird. I gave the guy my order, and asked him how long it would be. I thought he'd ask me where I live. But he already knew that. And what I'd ordered last time. Hell, he even knew my name."

There was a huge, round lodge built of crosscut logs. Circles of logs, in layers, in a great dome—high as the tallest trees. In the center was a huge bonfire. The smoke was wafting in clouds, all the way to the top of the rustic lodge, as far as the eye could see.

All around the fire there was dancing. Rows of dancers, like spokes of a wheel. They were circling the fire to the beat of a drum. A huge kettle drum of deerskin stretched across a hollowed log. The drumbeat was primal, like the rhythm of the heart. And, like the heart, the beat never varied. Only every now and then the sound grew twice as loud: WHOOM. WHOOM. WHOOM. WHOOM.

Hawk was clad in deerskin. He could see that, and the

colored beads and feathers they all wore. Beside him was a young girl, dressed in skins as he was but with more of the decorative feathers. Some of them were turquoise and they fluttered to her movements: toe-heel, toe-heel. Sometimes she'd spin around, arms extended like an eagle, and the feathers would fly out and float through the air. Hawk looked on as she was spinning, round and round.

As he watched the girl, he wanted to speak. But no sound came. All he could hear was the thrum of the drum. WHOOM/BOOM, WHOOM/BOOM, WHOOM/BOOM, WHOOM/BOOM. WHOOM. WHOOM. WHOOM. WHOOM.

He looked again: her lips were moving. Now he leaned closer to hear. And then he watched in awe as the young girl was transformed into a woman. She had full lips and dark hair, black as onyx. And then he saw, to his amazement, that she wore no clothes at all. As his eyes drifted down along her tan torso, he shuddered at the sight of her firm nipples, the color of mahogany, on swelling breasts. Now she drew close, her warm breasts pressed against his chest.

She was speaking again, and he strained to hear. Her voice was dreamlike.

"Hawk, do you ever believe you can see ahead?"

He shook his head and looked closely. His eyes were coming into focus.

"What I mean is," she was saying, "can you sense what's going to happen? Sometimes I think I can."

Hawk laughed and nodded knowingly. Then he rose up on an elbow to relish the sight of her. But as he felt his ardor rise, he suddenly stopped cold. He was lying limp, and couldn't do more. There'd been too much in the dream of his young cousin. He knew he wasn't ready for Cassy.

Now he glanced at the clock: almost seven o'clock. That late! He put some coffee on to brew as they showered and dressed in yesterday's gym clothes. It was not yet 7:30 when he pulled up outside the Hermitage. They ran in to pick up their work clothes where they'd left them before going to the gym. He was careful to turn off all the lights and lock the front door. There was no sign they'd been in.

But as he climbed in the car to drive Cassy back to her place, he looked up and there was Teresa in her red Mazda. Scanning the street for a parking place, a half block away.

Back in his office by nine o'clock, Hawk was leafing through some files when Todd walked in. "What's on the docket?" he asked as Hawk spun around, clutching a large folder. Todd nodded at the folder. "More 'strategic planning?'"

Todd's grin was inscrutable, and Hawk decided to play it straight. "More like going through some articles on crisis management. I haven't looked through this stuff for a while and something tells me I should be up on it. And, hey, I'm sorry about yesterday. Cassy should be here any minute."

Todd offered a sardonic smile. "I've heard it called a lot of things. But 'strategic planning'? Got to hand it to you, podner. And to Teresa for keeping me updated... By the way, Cassy's been here and gone. She came in before you showed up and I sent her out on assignment."

"Oh, yeah? What kind of assignment? I thought I was supervising her."

"Among your other duties, eh, podner?" Todd's grin was turning tighter. "Well, time is of the essence. I've got news releases going out to all the TV stations, and the video phones are due tomorrow. But we still have fifteen members of the Peak Society who haven't signed up for the program. Time for some sales calls, and who better than the best-looking Nanticoke on the planet?"

Hawk dropped the folder on his desk and leaned over it. "Okay, hold it! What are we selling here, tits and ass? What all did you tell her to say?"

"As little as possible," Todd snapped back. "We've got

the sound bite on the flyer. I just told her to hang around each member's office 'til they let her in. Then she hands the guy a flyer and asks him to sign up. And, of course, with a winning smile."

Todd turned on a dime and strode out.

16

Late September was a gorgeous time in Denver—before the skies would go gray, the winds would blow cold, and winter would come to camp on the doorstep, some time in mid-October. Hawk found himself out of the office a lot, taking advantage of the last, bright, crystalline days of fall.

He spent his days paying visits to community groups begging for bucks from Telwest. Since he hadn't heard anything more from Wally, he assumed he'd have to make decisions about funding proposals by himself.

Now it was midmorning on a crisp, sunlit day and he was off to visit a social service center in northeast Denver, a black and Hispanic part of town. There was some sort of special event being put on by the Police Athletic League, and they'd asked him to stop by.

On a whim, Hawk had called up Lance Rossiter, with the Broncos. Maybe this was a time to expose Benjie Green, that weird wide receiver, to the concept of community service.

Could Lance pick up Benjie and come out there?

"Sure," he'd said. "They don't practice till three o'clock. I'll get him out of bed and we'll be up. Do you think they can use him for some kind of TV spot? Maybe one where he doesn't have to say anything?"

Hawk said, "Let's hold off on that. We don't know what sort of event this is. I don't like to expose a client to the camera until we have a pretty good idea of what's going to happen."

"Well, he's a hot property right now," Lance exulted. "His agent told me there's a shoe company calling him. Maybe an endorsement deal."

Hawk said he'd seen the highlights of the game on Sunday. "It's not every day you snag six passes, one for a touchdown. But, talk about an exhibitionist. What a hot dog. That end-zone dance!"

As he drove along, Hawk wondered what sort of event he was headed for and how Benjie would fit in with the kids in the Police Athletic League.

More than that, he was wondering about Cassy. He hadn't seen her for a couple of days. She must be really humping on those sales calls. Either that or... Were they avoiding one another? He didn't like to think about that.

Nor about the fact he'd lost his safety net. The distance he'd kept between himself and any sort of commitment to a relationship. Teresa had been chiding him a couple of weeks ago. "Hawk, I saw you out at lunch with—okay, who was she? You know, you go through women like some people change clothes. And you've always got some new ones in the closet."

Well, come to think of it, he hadn't even called up any of them since Cassy had arrived in town. That made him nervous.

Yesterday, she'd left a research paper on his desk. He'd found it when he got back to the office, late in the afternoon. It was something about Stages of Buying Readiness. She must have done it for a course at Haskell and she was asking for his comments. The idea was that, when you're selling, you need to figure out how your client is thinking, where his head is:

- Unawareness of the services available
- Awareness of the services
- Comprehension of the services

- Interest in the services
- Desire for the services
- Willingness to take action to receive the services

His first reaction when he read it was to feel sorry for Cassy. All these courses in marketing, and where does she end up? Out on sales calls, working for a lout like Todd.

But something else caught his attention, and his eyes had gone wide as he'd re-read each line. All he could think of was his marketing strategies with women. Meeting them at each of these stages, overcoming objections, all the way up to his condo, and the consummation of the sale, the closing of the deal. It had been a science, with one after another, until Cassy came along and...

Oh, Jesus. Were they really related?

Thankfully, he found himself at the circular drive to the Clayton Center, a turn-of-the-century cluster of sandstone buildings at the corner of Martin Luther King and Colorado Boulevards. The center had been founded in 1910 as a charitable orphanage, designated by George Clayton in his will as a place to serve not just any orphans, but "poor white males." He'd left a generous endowment.

But with the Civil Rights Act of the sixties, the white-male business wouldn't wash. Some lawyers on the board had got the charter changed. Now, the kids who came here for all kinds of programs were all kinds of colors. Hawk loved coming out to the old orphanage. It was one of the few places he felt at home.

He parked behind a Victorian building with a big white turret and looked around for Lance. There he was, over on the grassy playground behind the admin building. He was standing there watching a group of maybe twenty youngsters. They were grade school aged, and they all wore royal blue T-shirts, no doubt compliments of the Police Athletic League.

The kids were having a great time and, as Hawk came near them, he felt buoyed by their laughter. They seemed to be practicing some kind of dance routine, and squealing like banshees as they tried to get the hang of it. He came up behind Lance and clapped him on the shoulder. His old running back turned to him with a grin, and pointed toward the festivities.

That's when Hawk recognized what was going on. It was Benjie Green, out there in the middle of the pack. In the bright, sunny day, the man sparkled. He had on a tailored leisure suit, suede and antelope tan. The suit set off the radiance of his deep, teak brown complexion. The sweat on the crown of his shaven head was glistening in the sun.

Benjie had reason to be working up a sweat. He was in motion out there in the middle of the group, gyrating to some self-invented rhythm as the kids all bopped around him, following along. There was a pendant hanging from a leather cord around his neck and it bounced against his thick chest to the beat.

It seemed whatever Benjie was doing here at Clayton, he'd come out dressed for the part. Hawk found himself rocking to the rhythm as Benjie repeated the riff time and again. He juked to the left, juked to the right. Took a stutter step and sashayed forward in a kind of shuffle. Finally, he bent his body at the waist, slapped his butt, and rose up to his full height, fluttering his fingers in the air.

Hawk could see the routine was taking hold. It was Benjie's end-zone dance, and more and more of the kids were getting it. To Hawk, a dance like this had always looked ridiculous in the middle of a game. But out here in the fresh grass of the playground, between the jungle gym and the swing set—why, Benjie was a natural.

"He seems to like children," Hawk said.

Lance nodded. "Hawk, this was a great idea. I mean, he's

been through that dance a dozen times. He loves those kids. And look, there's the TV crew. I'm glad they made it."

Hawk saw where he was pointing. There was a white van with a logo: "Sports on Six!" It had a transmitter on top.

"How'd they get here?" Hawk asked. He watched a spindly little guy in a white shirt and a bright orange tie directing a camera man in T-shirt and jeans. The camera was zooming in on Benjie as the impromptu dance rehearsal finally ground to a halt. The kids were crowding around the Broncos' wide receiver. Benjie was sweating profusely but grinning like he'd just won the lottery.

Hawk punched Lance on the shoulder. "How did they get here?" he repeated.

Lance turned to him with a sheepish grin. "Well, I couldn't see how it'd hurt," he told him. "Benjie's such a child. I figured he'd be good with kids. And he doesn't have to say..."

"Oh, my God," Hawk exploded. "I see what's going on. Quick, get in there and grab him. Get him outta here."

But it was too late. Hawk watched the white-shirted announcer take Benjie by he elbow. He led him to a second van, just in front of the TV vehicle. Hawk hadn't noticed it before, but he saw there'd been a tarpaulin covering the side. Now the tarp was coming off, as the announcer thrust a microphone in front of Benjie. He held a friendly arm around his shoulder and squared him up to face the camera, as the sign on the side of the van was revealed.

STADIUM FRANKS - ALL NATURAL

HOT DOG EATING CONTEST!

Lance stood transfixed as he watched his player being framed for the evening news: an icon for a hot dog sponsor.

As he pushed his way toward the announcer, Hawk ran a calculation of what was happening to Benjie. They'd open the spot with his hot-dog dance. And then, not only would he receive no compensation for being ridiculed this way, but he could also say good-bye to a gig for a shoe company, as well as any other lucrative endorsement.

Hawk got to the announcer just as he was starting his spiel. "Well, Benjie, that was some dance routine, and the kids sure enjoyed it..."

"A lot more than you will when I shove this fucking microphone down your throat," Hawk thundered as he grabbed the mike and threw the announcer off camera. He loomed over him, twirling the microphone like a yo-yo. "Down your throat or up your ass!" He threw it at him.

"Hey, watch out. That's our equipment!" the little guy screamed.

"Yeah, whatcha doon?" Benjie hollered. "I be gettin' some exposure."

"Benjie," Hawk said, "You are getting nothing but exploited. Now, go find Lance and get out of here. We'll get you the right kind of publicity—the kind that pays money."

Benjie's eyes brightened at the concept, and he turned to find Lance at his elbow.

Meanwhile, as the announcer scrambled to his feet, it seemed the camera was still rolling. "Hey, I know you," he whined at Hawk. He turned to the camera. "You're Hawk Kidree, ex-offensive lineman. Isn't that what you were? Well, folks, as you can see, he's still plenty offensive.

"And here's what's amazing. A guy like this? He thinks he can make a living in public relations. For Sports on Six, this is Bart Barrabee."

Hawk had taken two steps inside the Hermitage when Todd came pounding down the hall. His face was flushed, and he was panting.

"Teresa said you were coming up the steps," he sputtered.

Hawk looked at him impassively. "It's nice to be noticed."

"Well, I guess you were, from what I hear. The guys at Channel Six just called. I heard all about what happened. The only good part was they asked if I wanted the name of our firm in the story."

"I assume you told 'em to go ahead," Hawk responded. "You're always quoting P.T. Barnum: 'There's no bad publicity.'"

Todd glowered at him for a half minute. "What on earth would lead you to assault a television reporter? Club him down! They said you hit him with his microphone—live and on camera!"

Hawk was silent for a moment as he looked at Todd, surveyed him up and down. "Well, it was the fullback on my college team. Plus a young kid too naïve to handle all the attention he's getting. But I don't think I could explain it to you."

He turned and walked back out the door. As he headed down the sidewalk, he glanced back at the window of the reception room. He saw Teresa standing there. He thought he saw her grinning.

Hawk turned up at the Wynkoop about 7:30. It was past time for the news at five and well before the ten o'clock edition. He headed for a back booth and ordered a ration of pub food: shepherd's pie and a pint of Railyard Ale. Then he set out a legal pad he'd brought along, and started writing.

It was a habit he'd cultivated in college, and lately he'd got back to it. Writing was something that could totally absorb him, and when the waitress brought him his frothing glass of beer he scarcely noticed. Whatever he was working on—an article, or a journal entry—didn't seem to matter.

Tonight, he was intent on it, trying to find some distance from the spirits of the strange world that surrounded him. He'd filled half a dozen pages when he felt a nudge and saw a shadow fall across his pad.

"Is this an open booth, or by invitation only?"

"Oh, hi, Cassy. Come, sit down."

"You're not signing autographs?"

Hawk gave an open grin and shook his head. He felt a wave of kinship once again, as though sex didn't altogether matter. Cassy was dressed for the business world and as beautiful as ever. But she appeared to be exhausted.

Hawk waved for the waitress and pointed to his glass. Cassy allowed as how she hadn't eaten, but wasn't hungry yet.

"So, you saw the evening news?" he asked.

"I did. Do you want to talk about it?" The waitress brought her beer, and Cassy took a long draw.

Hawk shook his head: no.

Cassy said, "Well, I saw what you did, and I think I understood."

Hawk's dinner arrived, and he asked for a second fork. He set it between them.

They sat in silence for a long time as Hawk attacked the shepherd's pie. Cassy drained her beer and ordered another. Hawk got her some peanuts. "You'd better eat something," he told her.

The brew pub was quiet, early in the evening—just now and then a click of balls from the pool table. Finally Cassy pointed to the legal pad. "Okay if I look at what you were writing?"

"It is if you take that fork and eat something."

"Jesus!" she fumed. "You'd think you were my cousin or something."

She crinkled her nose as she saw him cringe. "Well, you know what they say: if they can't take a fuck, joke 'em."

Hawk gave a start. He said, "I think you're getting drunk."

"Oh, all right. There, I put down two mouthfuls. Now, lemme see what you've been writing."

There was a droning sound of talking heads from the television over the bar, chewing over the news. Did O.J. really do it? And what about the Clintons? The Whitewater affair. The suicide of Vincent Foster. Speaking of affairs, what about Hillary and Vincent? Did they ever do it?

Finally, she looked up and said, "That's really interesting. I guess I should have known you could write—from all the way back in college. But this is good. The new e-conomy. Based on selling experiences, right?"

"Vicarious experience," he added. "Like spectator sports. Not just watching the guy catch a touchdown pass, but knowing how he felt when he caught it. And spectator sex. Add that in."

He told about the nympho coeds in the hot tub, on television at the resort. "I mean, it makes sense. A culture where people can no longer live fully in the present. They don't trust it. They're always on the lookout for something more."

"And you're saying the economy needs that."

Hawk nodded. "It's a market for selling new experiences. As long as you can keep offering them something more."

Cassy said, "Hold that thought. I need to go to the john."

"When you come back," Hawk said, "for Christ's sake will you eat something? No offense, but you're starting to look pale."

She walked back to the booth with a thoughtful expression and dutifully picked up her fork. "So, where does the video phone fit in all this? You know, I was thinking about the woman on the screen, whacking off in Wally's office.

"Whoops, sorry. I should have blushed again. I hadn't

intended to show you that side of me—not yet, anyhow. You know, you can take the girl out of the gambling casino, but you can't take..."

Hawk said, "It's pretty hard to shock me."

"Maybe so. But that look on your face!"

They sat for a while in silence. Cassy finished the shepherd's pie and went up to the bar. She brought them back more beers. "So, what about my question? Do you think there's a connection?"

"I've been thinking about that, Cassy. And I realize maybe I haven't given this stuff enough thought."

"You've got that straight, Cochise. You know, the last couple of days—here, I've been making five or six sales calls a day. It's damn hard work, and I need some support. And I've hardly even seen you."

"I read your paper and it made some sense. But I don't know anything about this. I can't teach you to sell."

"I'm not looking for you to help me, Hawk. I just..." She took another swallow of beer and began to sputter. He offered her his napkin and she swiped it out of his hand. Then she used it to dab her eyes.

"I just want you to be involved in what we're doing. I mean, you turn the whole thing over to Todd the Clod. You let him run it. You let him tell me what to do. Do you even know who owns these damn video phones? You don't stand up..."

"Cassy, hold it. You saw the news, right? So, did you see what I did to that guy on television? That's why I walk away from Todd. My God, can you imagine..."

A few heads were turning at the bar and some couples were taking up the tables and booths around them. "Let's hold it down," Hawk told her.

"All right. But at least let me tell you what's going on—or show you." Cassy set her attache case on the bench beside her and clicked it open. She drew out a fax sheet and handed it to Hawk.

He took it as he glanced up at the clock. It was 9:45. They needed to be heading out of here pretty soon unless he wanted to bask in his celebrity on the ten o'clock news.

"So, what's this?" he muttered. "Just a lot of names, addresses, and telephone numbers."

"Well, look at the top," said Cassy. "Here, compare this to the other one." She handed him another fax sheet. "They're two lists of prospects."

Hawk studied the two documents. "Well, one of them seems to have an office address and phone number. The other has a home address and phone. Right?"

"Now, look at the top line." Cassy showed him.

"One of them says 'Peak Society,' which is what we're working on. And the one with the home phones is P-e-e-k. Okay, so it's misspelled. Is that it?"

"It is, except for the party sending it," Cassy told him. "For the Peak Society, it's the president of the group. I forget his name. But for the Peek Society, it's some guy named Vern Warner, at Telwest."

"Vern Warner." Hawk thought a minute. "Todd's buddy, the CIO... But what difference does it make?"

"Well, in the one case, I'm arranging to see these Peak Society members in their offices, during business hours. But I called up a couple of guys on the other list, and they wanted to meet in a bar. I think this is a different deal, and it's not part of our arrangement," Cassy said.

"Hey, it's ten minutes till news time," Hawk said. "Would you like to continue this stimulating discussion over at my place?"

Cassy gave a quizzical expression. "I'm not so sure, Cuz. I saw the way you looked at me back there. Maybe not in the state you're in."

"Well, one other thing then," Hawk said, slowly. "This is going back some. It's something I've been meaning to ask you. Do you remember if you and I were ever together at a powwow? I mean, way back. Say, when you were a kid. I think we might have been dancing."

She drained her beer and thought for several moments. She nodded and began smiling. "I was maybe ten," she said slowly. "You would have been eighteen. I think we were doing the eagle dance. And, yeah, I remember. Oh, I was so proud, Hawk. So proud of our kinship, so proud to be your…

"Hey, Hawk, what's wrong?" She got up from the booth and looked down at him. "Oh, my God, I did it again. Here, I was going to show you a few of my moves. And my feathers."

17

Hawk spent a restless night, waking and worrying. What was his future with Cassy? He knew he couldn't be lover/mentor/cousin to this woman—all these things—and she knew it as well. In the middle of the night, he gave up trying to sleep and took a seat out on the living room couch. In the darkness, he gazed down at the far end, where Cassy had sat. For a long time, he grappled with his gunny sack of conflicted feelings. His mind was racing, getting nowhere.

Finally, he closed his eyes and let himself be led back into the dream: the drumbeat and the dance in the round. He listened to the drum, to his heartbeat. He closed his eyes, let the rhythm surround him.

When he opened his eyes, he blinked at the daylight. Though he was still on the couch, he must have slept most of the night. As he gathered his thoughts, he wondered whether anything had changed. Who knew what the future held with Cassy? But still, he felt an odd sense of confidence. Something felt different, in the wake of the dream.

He seemed to be seeing more clearly, breathing more slowly. He thought about that, brewing his coffee. Perhaps there was a way he could help Cassy. He decided to get dressed up and drive by Wally's office.

The drive in wasn't bad. Having slept till almost eight o'clock, he'd missed rush hour. There was no telling what else he'd missed at the office. But he felt full of energy this morning, and gave a modest whoop as he found a parking place just a few blocks from Wally's place.

He slipped four quarters into a parking meter and set out for the Telwest building through the cold, stone canyons of downtown Denver. Generally, he avoided this part of the city: a jumble of buildings from various boom times when the locals had had money. It had none of the red brick warmth of lower downtown. But today this flotsam of concrete glowed a little.

What was it that had got into him this morning? For an instant, he thought he caught a glimpse of Manito in a shaft of sunlight glancing off a pushcart on the sidewalk. The giver god must be smiling. Or, was it just the bald head of the old guy selling breakfast burritos?

For whatever reason, he seemed more open to the world as he worked his way through the Telwest lobby toward the elevators. The lobby was full of workers coming on at nine o'clock, and he watched them as they milled about. He noticed the numbers on their badges. There were the 3s: white-collar middle managers. And now and then a full-fledged 4, a higher-up at Wally's level.

Today, he paid attention to these people.

How did they get into work like this? Did anyone ever set out to work for the phone company? To spend their days devising systems to distribute telephone directories, to get quarters out of pay phones? Or was Telwest just a fate that had befallen them?

He could envision an exchange at a bus stop or a bar. "So, you're looking for a job? I've got an uncle down at Telwest. Call him up. They're hiring."

Now this bunch of fall-in-line bureaucrats was supposed to become high stakes players in advanced telecommunications, the come-and-get-it industry of the nineties. It was like fashioning a race car from a station wagon.

The elevator, full of Telwest workers, gave a "ping" at

every floor where they got on or off. But he noticed that they all left before he did. There must be damn few workers on the upper floors. Hawk knew that the first people they laid off were managers. Along with blue sky technoids such as Wally. The guys who collected quarters from the pay phones stayed on.

Finally the bell rang for the thirty-second floor and the doors opened to Wally's department. Hawk stepped out into the foyer and gave a start. The entire floor was swarming with men in dark green work clothes. Some of them were pushing trains of swivel chairs while others loaded desks onto dollies or boxed-up computers. Wally was being moved out, lock, stock, and modem.

Hawk headed for the far corner that had been Wally's office, a bit self-conscious in his suit and tie and briefcase amid the sea of dark green movers. As Hawk approached, he could see that the furniture was still set up in there.

But the office was vacant. He stepped inside and looked around. On one corner of a desk was a square-cut device with a big screen, which he took to be a video phone. He wondered how many of the damn things Wally had ordered. Todd had mentioned something about a delivery. Now he wondered why he hadn't heard of that. Wasn't he supposed to be the liaison to Wally?

There was a large white board on one wall of the office, with two parallel flow charts scrawled out by magic markers. The charts were in different colors, one black the other blue. But their components seemed about the same. At the bottom of each one was a box labeled "Address Book." Perhaps that was the most complex part of the system. Then Hawk noticed the headings for the flow charts. One was labeled "Peak Society," the other "Peek Society."

What was that: some kind of geek joke? Then he remembered his conversation with Cassy.

He found himself searching the office, but for what he

wasn't sure. There was a two-tier file tray on the right hand corner of Wally's desk, opposite the video phone, and he began leafing through it. One tray was labeled "Outgoing Faxes." He was sifting through a sheaf of papers when a line on the top sheet caught his eye. The message had been sent to his own firm: "Mountain High Communications."

Hawk plopped down in Wally's chair. It was a brief note, apparently meant for him. But he hadn't seen it until now. He glanced at the next page: instructions for operating the video phone. Hawk had just started reading when a voice like gravel growled behind him.

"Who the hell are you, sport? You ain't Wally."

Hawk turned around in his chair very slowly, the faxes in hand. A squat, swarthy man in dark green work clothes stood glowering at him from the door to the office. He was clutching a clipboard. He peered at Hawk.

"Hey, what the fuck! You're going through his correspondence?"

Hawk rose to his feet and walked across the office. He looked down at the man. There was a title sewn on his lapel. "Supervisor, Sol."

Hawk gave a long look at him. Riffling through his deck of ethnic role cards, he chose tribal black. In a deep, gutteral tone, he droned, "Mmm."

Then, "Sol, you're astute. That's just what I am doing. As a matter of fact, I'm looking for some documents: official correspondence."

Sol took the measure of Hawk, his size and his suit. Wide-eyed, he looked him up and down. "Well, they said something about a lawyer. I guess that's you, huh?"

"Mmm."

"Well, just let me know when you're gonna be leaving."

"There's one other thing, Sol. I need to check on where the office furnishings are going. Mmm."

Sol squinted at him, clutching his clipboard tighter. "So,

you're his lawyer. And you don't know where he's goin'?" He took a step back out through the door. "You wait here, Champ. There's something I gotta do."

Hawk spun around to Wally's desk as he flipped open his briefcase. He grabbed the entire stack of Wally's faxes and stuffed them inside.

As he left Wally's office, Hawk eyed the cavernous work area outside. With the cubicles dismantled, the place looked like a vacant factory floor. He spotted Sol, over by the far window. He was dialing up a cellular phone and, as he held it to his ear, he looked up in Hawk's direction.

Hawk headed for the elevators, started to run. The security guards would be here any minute. Then he stopped and took a moment to think about a plan. He headed down a hall, looking for a door to the stairwell. He found it and started down. Three floors, then back to the elevators.

He pressed the button down, and waited an eternity. Again, he felt an impulse to run—up, down, anywhere—but he stood in place and tried to quiet his breathing. Finally, the elevator arrived. Thank God, it was empty. He pushed a button for garage, hoping no one else would come on board. The elevator skipped the lobby and opened on a subterranean floor marked P-1.

He got off and found the staircase up to the lobby.

As he opened the door, he saw three or four security guards scrambling around the elevators. But no one was watching the stairs from the garage. He breathed a sigh of relief, turned away, and walked out the side door onto 17th Street and into the hubbub of the financial district. Two blocks down the street, he was immersed in the crowds, a world away from Telwest.

He caught sight of a coffee bar and decided to stop in. He took his coffee to a table back in the corner, sat down, and took a sip as he unzipped his briefcase. Leafing through the faxes, he scanned the correspondents. Several of them were under the same logo: The Summit Group. There was an address on Yosemite Drive, down in the Denver Technological Center, south of town.

It was a popular site for corporate headquarters, and Hawk recognized the company. They ran a chain of hotels—as a matter of fact, one of them was the resort where Natalie worked—along with a couple of local sports franchises. Word was they were getting into other aspects of the entertainment field, broadcasting pay-for-view programs into the hotel rooms. Now you could dial up all sorts of entertainment, all in your hotel room. He remembered the porn movie on the TV that night at Natalie's place. Spectator sports. Spectator sex.

Something else came to mind—a conversation he'd overheard a week or so ago at the gym. Two middle-aged guys wheezing through their miles on the treadmill. Gasping out data on trends in the hotel industry. And what he'd picked up was surprising. It seemed the Summit Group had been pulling in half their revenue from one source: transmitting soft-porn movies into the hotel rooms.

The experience industries. The new e-conomy. Might make an op-ed piece for the *Chronicle*. Maybe he'd run the idea by Branscomb some day.

He turned back to the faxes, found another message to Mile High Communications. What was this?

> Hawk,
>   No time to get together. It's all going so damn fast. Bottom line is, they're moving me out, reassigning me. And I can't say where. It's part of the deal, along with a three-month contract extension. Seems like somebody up there likes me.
>   But still no staff. Any programming, I'll be doing

it. Even Gladys is gone. Remember the Office Mom? But I got her another assignment with the new boss. Should be right up her alley!

Now, I've got you a hundred video phones, plus a couple for you guys on the side. Peak Society members can use them for two months free. Then you're on your own with Telwest. Cut whatever kind of deal you can. Delivery costs are covered, and you get your consulting fees. Same retainer, but only two months more.

After that, I'd say you're in the video phone business. Been good working with you, but now I'm outta here. Another project. As a matter of fact, a couple of 'em. Big ones. So long, Hawk—it's been fun.

Wally

P.S. These video phones work good except for the address book. Been having a bitch of a time with it.

Well, that was Wally, back in the hunt. Hawk felt a sense of relief to see his old client on top of his game. Now he had something to be excited about, and that was good. Wally's life was pretty much his job. But what would he be doing, and for whom? Had he really changed employers?

There was a spider web slowly forming in one corner of the coffee bar. He watched it for a moment, sipping his coffee. Something about the web caught his interest. It was the idea of entanglement, the way it could capture everything in sight.

He peered at the web through the dust that swirled in the morning light. In his mind's eye he envisioned a very large web, encompassing all of Denver. Who was spinning that one? Who would be the next one caught?

Hawk drained his coffee in one gulp as another question

came to the fore. This one was more pressing and it started to gurgle in his gut. Why hadn't he got that fax from Wally?

There was something different about the Hermitage as Hawk walked through the door. It was a poster, two-feet tall, on the front door: "JUST DO SOMETHING." A tagline at the bottom said: "Telwest Advanced Technologies." He found another just like it tacked up over the reception desk. In fact, there were posters plastered all over their office suite. They were black with bright blue letters.

A strange young woman sat at the reception desk. Long blonde hair. A Nordic type, like Todd. She looked up at Hawk and started to say something, but the telephone rang. Then a second call came in, and a third. Again and again, she recited her spiel: "Mile High Communications. How can I help you?" He stood by the desk and waited as she fumbled with the mechanics of putting one call on hold while answering the next. Two of the calls were for Todd, the other for Cassy. She said both of them were out, and sent the callers into voice mail.

Finally, the young woman turned back to Hawk with a shy smile and a sigh of exhaustion. "I'm Laurie," she said, "and I bet you're Mr. Kidree. Teresa told me to look for a football player."

"It's 'Hawk,'" he said, extending his hand. "How long have you..."

Teresa came scurrying around the corner, carrying a stack of flyers. Her head was turned and she was panting. "He told me it goes here," she said, and pointed to a wood-paneled wall. A man in overalls materialized behind her. He was hauling a vinyl banner, six feet wide. It, too, was black with bright blue letters. "THE NEXT BIG THING," it read, and there was a picture of a video phone. The man set the sign on a side chair and went off to get a ladder.

Teresa turned back. "Oh, *hola*, Hawk. So, you've met

Laurie. You know, I had to get some help, all this product launch and such. The video phones are in and they're being delivered. You'll see UPS guys running in and out. Oh, and you had a fax, but Todd picked it up. He's calling on TV stations. Cassy's out seeing prospects."

She paused for breath. "In case you didn't know," she added with a sly smile. "And, hey, I don't know why he took off with your fax, *amigo*."

Hawk shook his head. "So, how do you like this life in the fast lane?"

She screwed up her face. "It pays the rent."

"Well, I'm going to barricade myself in my office," Hawk said. "When you see Todd, please tell him I was looking for him. And tell him I wasn't grinning."

"So I will. But one thing, Hawk." She looked aside. "Lately, I have seen you smile. I think I know why. And it makes me feel so good."

There was a screech from around the corner. "Say, where do you want this, lady?" The guy in overalls was back, pushing what appeared to be a four-foot replica of a video phone on a dolly.

Teresa pointed to a corner of the reception room. "I think that goes over to the demo at the Wynkoop tonight. Let's put it over there for now," she said.

She turned back to Hawk and wiped her brow. "And one more thing, *mi amigo*, before we get back on the fast track. I want you to know this proverb."

He looked at her aghast. "Another one?"

"Now listen closely, and say after me. *Todo el mundo.*"

"*Todo el mundo.*"

"*Todo el mundo es mi primo!*"

Hawk reached for a message pad and wrote it down. "You know '*primo*'?"

He said, "I hear the Hispanic guys calling one another that all the time. Isn't it something like 'cousin'?"

Teresa said, "That's very good. *Que bueno*! Now, '*todo el mundo.*' That's 'all the world,' but it's our way of saying 'everybody.' Now, translate it for me: '*Todo el mundo es mi primo.*'"

"It loses something in translation," Hawk said. "But I guess it's 'everyone's my cousin.'"

She gave Hawk a long look with a warm smile. "'*Todo el mundo es mi primo.*' Think about it, cousin."

He took Wally's faxes back to his office. A minute ago, he'd been hell bent for leather, hot on the trail of whatever Todd was up to. Intent on going over the rest of the messages he'd purloined. But Teresa had thrown him off the track. His head was spinning at the proverb she'd taught him, and why.

Now there was something else to consider.

He noticed a big manila envelope in the middle of his desk. "Hawk," it read, and he recognized the handwriting. He stuck Wally's faxes in a file drawer, took a deep breath, and opened the envelope with a twinge of trepidation. There was a note inside, and a drawing.

> Hawk,
>
> What do you say to an actual date? Tonight. Drinks and dinner, 5:00 at the Wynkoop. But first, check out this chart. (You show me yours, and I'll show you mine.) Plus one other thing. Can you come up with something I can tell these Peak Society guys other than that this video phone is "the next big thing?" They need a reason to sign up and I can't bring myself to say that. Help!
>
> Cassy

He read the note three or four times. The chart was in the form of a family tree. It went back three generations, to her grandparents. What would his look like? Where would they connect? He knew what was at stake, and it made him shiver.

He went out and got some coffee. He tried to think of what to do next. Forget the faxes. He couldn't lay into Todd if he wasn't here. What about the chart? He couldn't face that yet. Maybe tonight, over a couple of beers, at dinner. Could they make a game of it? That wasn't the way it felt right now.

Hawk put the chart back in the envelope and switched on his computer. If nothing else, he could work on some writing. And he had an idea that might help Cassy.

18

It was another notion that had been simmering in his brain for the past several days, and it felt good to write it down. So much so that he wondered again if he missed journalism. The idea came with a headline, "Negative Tech," and the idea became so vivid that it almost seemed to write itself on the screen.

The gist of it was that progress can take two forms. Sometimes a discovery adds an ingredient to our lives that wasn't there before. Take video games, laser surgery, space shots to the moon.

But there's another kind of progress he called "negative tech." These are inventions that deduct something from our lives. They relieve us of what we didn't want to do in the first place. The maintenance-free townhouse. The TV dinner you don't prepare. The car finish you never have to wax.

Which brings us to the organization for people who don't have time for meetings. It's all made possible by the latest advance in telecom technology. The video phone, and the Peak Society. The club that never meets!

Hm, not bad, he thought. Like "the new e-conomy," it might make a column for Branscomb. He ran off what he'd written; he'd show it to Cassy tonight.

Then, on an impulse, he called up Art. He'd seen him only the day before, but it had been some time since he'd talked with him about his newspaper column. They seemed to avoid talking about the paper, since Hawk's hasty exit from the newsroom. And Branscomb didn't enjoy kibitzing about his column, which always threatened to dominate his life.

"You know, lots of people envy the guy who has a column," he'd once confided to Hawk. "How expressive, cathartic. But they don't know what it's like, cranking this stuff out over and over again. I tell you, it's like being married to a nymphomaniac. Every time you think you're done, it's time to start again."

Sometimes his syntax got a bit fuzzy, and Hawk knew the editors got on him for that. Those were the days he found himself half in the bag and on deadline, pounding out his text with Rusty Nails, his favorite libation.

When he reached Art by phone, Hawk was glad to find him at his desk, more or less clear-headed and free for lunch. It was a half-mile over to the Chronicle from lower downtown, but a nice day to walk, and the paper wasn't far from Branscomb's favorite watering hole, the Denver Press Club.

The paper maintained moderate security operations to snag the occasional, enraged subscriber; you were supposed to sign in at the front desk. But the receptionist recognized Hawk and waved him toward the elevators. As he stepped out into the press room, he walked into a jumble of memories. What a job! There was the excitement of seeing your copy in print, your name in a by-line. Plus the pride you felt, telling people you were a journalist. It sounded a hell of a lot more reputable than being in public relations.

But, then, there was the pay; he'd made half again as much in PR than at the newspaper. And add to that the confinement of spending your days hooked up to a telephone and a computer—calling up sources, knocking out copy.

The newsroom at the Chronicle was a huge, gray place that might have been designed as a warehouse. And the reporters were just as nondescript. Most of them wore sweaters and jeans. They never went out except for lunch.

As he looked out over the horde of journalists, Hawk thought the whole scene looked a lot like an undergraduate study hall, the reporters like aging students. Which, in a sense, they were. Reporters weren't quite fully adult. They never initiated anything, but spent their lives recounting what other people did.

Yet, there was the excitement of the breaking story.

"Hawk!" He made his way toward a bank of windows where a long arm in a checkered shirt was waving. Here and there along the way, a reporter looked up to acknowledge him with a nod of the head and a grin. One of them put his hand to his throat and tugged at an imaginary tie. Hawk shielded his eyes in mock embarrassment. To some extent, this felt like home.

"Do I need a break," Art exclaimed. "Two hours to deadline, and look at what I've got." Hawk glanced at the computer monitor. There were only two paragraphs of text, less than half a screen.

He walked Branscomb over to the Press Club, wondering if he'd wind up lugging him back. He resolved to keep the lunch sober and succinct. But it was a quarter to twelve, and the columnist was overdue. Hawk ordered them each a Rusty Nail and felt his stomach cramp at the first swig of the sweet, acrid mixture of Scotch and drambuie.

As a newspaperman, he was clearly out of shape.

"So, what's up? You said you had something for me."

Hawk watched Art drain his first drink. He'd always marveled that such a free-wheeling individual could have played the hands-to-the-vest role of psychiatrist. Perhaps Art had always been fascinated by the vagaries of human emotions, but hadn't had the discipline to sit still and help people sort through them hour after hour, keeping them in place.

Art sat silent for a while, encouraging his friend to talk. As always, it was easy to envision Art Branscomb as a therapist, albeit one who now and then would fling an arm in the air for another Rusty Nail. Hawk began to tell him about the Peak Society project. But he didn't say much about Wally, and nothing at all about his memo: his doubts about how the video phone would work, his comment on the address-book feature.

Now the two were on a different playing field, and there were some items of information he would withhold. It was a cardinal rule in public relations: never tell a journalist anything you don't want to see in print.

When Hawk was finished, Art had a few things to say about Telwest and the local economy. "Video phone or whatever—you know they've got to come up with something. All those other phone companies are eating their lunch, cutting into their telephone business, year after year. That's deregulation for you.

"And we've just begun to see the layoffs. Have you ever heard the stats? I'll tell you, the psychiatrists know 'em by heart. For every two percent increase in unemployment, illness, suicide, domestic violence, murder—go up by four percent. Every increase of three percent, it all goes up nine. It's a geometric progression." He shuddered and sank into silence, then ordered another drink.

Hawk waited a few minutes, sharing the silence. Sometimes he wondered if the ex-psychiatrist had cared too much about people to listen to their problems hour after hour, cold sober. Finally, he spoke up.

"Look, Art, I brought you something I wrote up this morning—some notes on something else I think the video phone means. That's when I thought of calling you; I'd be interested in what you think."

Branscomb leaned back and looked at him with narrowed eyelids. Hawk knew what he was thinking. There was no end to the ploys these public relations people would try on him, to get their promotions in print. But Art knew him too well for that. And, besides, he was drawing a blank with his column.

Art picked up the notes on Negative Tech and read them over. He peered at Hawk a second time, over his eyeglasses. Then he put down his drink and signaled for a bowl of soup and a cup of strong, black coffee. With an hour and a half to deadline, he had a column for the afternoon edition.

As he hiked back to his office, Hawk had time to wonder about what he'd done. It was one thing to dash off those notes on the video phone for Cassy. But to turn them loose in a major daily was another matter. Suppose the damn video phone didn't work right. That was one concern. And lurking somewhere in the back of his mind was another. But what was it?

Rounding the corner to the Hermitage, an image slowly came into focus. It was the woman Cassy said she had seen on the screen in Wally's office. He thought of that phrase on the board, "The Peek Society." And also on the new list of prospects from Todd's friend, Vern Warner. Again, "The Peek Society." That had to be more than a misprint.

Suddenly, he wondered what Todd might know.

He looked up to see his partner just ahead, heading up the stairs to the Hermitage. Hawk sprinted a couple of steps and grabbed him by the collar. "This will be short, but we need a meeting," he told Todd and he marched him in past the reception desk all the way back to his office. Laurie, the new receptionist, stared wide-eyed at the procession.

Hawk shut the door to his office and sat Todd down on a side chair. "Okay, there's good news and bad news," he told him.

"Well, I can imagine which you'll lead with," Todd

grumbled. "And I suppose this is about your fax." He reached in his briefcase. "I'll give it back."

Hawk held out his hand. There was no point in letting him know he'd already read it.

"There's a reason I took it," Todd went on. "I needed some way to charge the video phone deliveries to Telwest. Either that or use our company credit card, which, you may not be aware, is maxed out. When I read the fax from Wally, I figured I could use it as a work authorization order. And it worked!"

His eyes got bright and he flashed his trademark grin. "The TV stations loved the Peak Project. You know KGO, Channel 9, Live at Five? Thank God you didn't go after their guy. The station manager's a member of the Peak Society, and he hooked up his video phone right away. Said something about dialing up for the first time live, on air."

Todd nattered on about his calls on the other broadcasters. He'd left a big black poster with each of them as a backdrop: THE NEXT BIG THING.

Hawk waited till he stopped to catch his breath. Then he handed him his notes on "negative technology." Todd looked through them with a puzzled frown, grappling with the abstraction. But when Hawk explained that Art Branscomb had picked up the idea for a column, his partner was ecstatic.

"I tell you, we've hit it—turned the corner," he exclaimed. "We're in business! I sent out a blast fax this morning to every member of the Peak Society. Told 'em all to turn on their video phones at five o'clock sharp. 'It's Happy Hour,' that's what I told 'em. 'But you don't have to leave home. It's Family Time, as well. Bring the wife and kids in. It's an experience they'll never forget. Just dial up the address book and...'"

"And what?" Hawk interjected. "Didn't you read the fax from Wally?"

"Well, most of it—scanned it." Todd paused to peruse the sheet in his hand. As he read along to the postcript on Wally's problems with the address book, two webs like crows' feet showed faintly along his eyelids. He started to get up, but Hawk pushed him back down.

"Todd, there's something I need to ask you. If you're up to it. You look a little pale, there, *Kimosabe*."

Todd shook his head. He squinted as he tried to grin, but his mouth was cinching into a tight line.

"The Peak Society. Not P-E-E-K. That's what you're supposed to be marketing, according to our agreement. With the hundred video phones Wally sent us. Half of which, you'll note, are mine."

Hawk felt his anger rising as he stared down at Todd, his partner suddenly submissive. The anger was involuntary, gut level, and it was growing into rage. He stepped away from Todd, walked around behind his desk, and sat down. But, still, he leaned forward. His eyes were blazing.

"Cassy gets some new prospects, from the Peek list—that's P-E-E-K, courtesy of your boy, Vern Warner—and where is it these guys want to get together? Not in their offices, like the others. They want to meet in a bar.

"Hey, Todd, I suppose you're glad to see I'm finally taking an interest in the business end of things. So, maybe you could tell me. Who are these dudes on the other list? Where did you get their names? And one more thing, if you don't mind, while we're at it. What the fuck is going on?"

Todd fumbled with the fax from Wally. He held it out at arm's length as he perused it, squinting at the paper like a sacred scroll. Hawk knew he was stalling for time.

Finally, Todd blurted out, "You'd have to ask Vern. Oh, right. I know, I never introduced you. But, you know, I sure can."

"And just what has Vern told you on this subject?"

"Not much. It's something about this new technology. Caller ID. If you're selling something, people call in. You build a list of who calls in. I guess that's how he got his... Honest to God, Hawk. That's all I know."

"Okay, so let's imagine there are two products. The one Cassy and I have known about. And this other one—the mystery list. And a technology that's still pretty dicey. Here's my second question. What's the hurry? Why the rush to market? Have you even thought about that?"

Todd sat hunched down with his head cocked. He scratched his neck and looked up with a quizzical expression. "Vern said something about an earnings report, end of quarter," he mumbled. "Far as I know, that's all they told him."

He fumbled in his pocket for an antacid.

19

Cassy took the call in the reception room of Stern and Harris, an upscale, downtown law office. She'd been waiting to see Arthur Stern, the senior partner, for an hour and had thumbed through all the magazines more than once. A typical day of cooling her heels in one anteroom after another—a reminder that this tedious business of outside sales was not what she'd gone back to school for. Today had been especially bad. Eight damn calls and not one conversation. She hadn't got in to see anybody. But at least it was her last assignment of the day.

She went back to a business magazine and turned to an article on something called "consultative sales." It was about approaching a prospect in the role of consultant. "Get deep into his business," the author advised. "Present yourself as a problem-solver. Understand his needs before…"

The receptionist called her name. She was wanted on the phone. She walked over to the front desk and picked up the receiver. At first there was nothing but silence on the line. Then a stammering. It was Wally.

He gave her an address down in the Denver Tech Center, south of town. Cassy had heard of the DTC, a cluster of modern office buildings surrounded by open fields, but had never been there. Wally told her which exit to take off the expressway and asked her to leave right then. There was a client in the offices of The Summit Group: an individual more vital to their project than the lawyer she'd been waiting for. His name was Granger Rowe, and it sounded vaguely familiar. Maybe he was another member of the Peak Society who was reluctant to sign up for the video phone.

As Cassy wound her way through the tangled streets of downtown Denver toward the freeway, she glanced at the clock on the dashboard of her car. It was not yet four o'clock. There should be enough time to give her sales pitch and get back to the Wynkoop to hook up with Hawk at five. She'd tried calling him from the law office, but he was out. And of course it was not like him to carry a cellular phone, much less a pager.

She exited on Yosemite and soon found herself in a maze of tree-lined parkways, surrounded by a battlement of office buildings that seemed to have been designed by the same school of architects—an outfit that must have specialized in Midwestern junior high schools. She had an address and tried following the signs, but the names of the streets and the numbering systems kept changing. Finally, she spotted a big, gold sign outside a barren, brown building a couple of stories high. The sign read: The Summit Group.

Cassy pulled around back into a parking lot, and walked into yet another reception room. Number nine of the day. This one served the entire building. The Summit Group was the only tenant. As she sat and waited for Granger Rowe, she toyed with the name and remembered where she'd heard it—somewhere around Telwest.

Finally, a door swung open at the far end of the lobby, and a young woman with a mane of tawny, red hair and a practiced smile came up to greet her. Would she like a soft drink? "No, thank you." But a pint of red ale would do fine, she reflected. It was about the color of the woman's hair.

She entered a cavernous room with a desk and chairs in the center of it. There was a green banker's lamp on the desk, but the rest of the room was in darkness. As her eyes became accustomed to the dim light, she saw that a man was seated behind the desk. Strange, this place was too large for an office. He motioned her to a side chair and rose to shake her hand. The fellow was rotund; it was the first thing she noticed about him.

"Good afternoon," he said in a big, round tone. "I'm Granger Rowe."

As she started to speak, suddenly a spotlight came on and shone directly in her eyes. She blinked for a moment as a myriad of circles started popping. "Sorry," he said. "It's something we need to do, just for a moment... So, then, what brings you down to see me?"

She gathered her wits and looked below the light with a smile. The sooner she started this, the quicker it'd be over. "Hello," she said, "My name is Cassandra Harmon. I'm here on behalf of the Peak Society. Have you heard about the video phone? I'd like you to know about it."

At that, the spotlight was shut off and Granger Rowe got up from his chair. "That was excellent," he exclaimed, leaning over the desk till he was looming over her. "Even though I know all about the video phone. And the Peak Society, too: both versions." He gave a snide laugh.

"Wally told me you were very professional." He was ogling her hair, her face and neck and arms: her complexion. He turned to his assistant. He said, "Allison, would you take Ms. Harmon back to the dressing room? What is it, thirty minutes to product launch?" He gave a kind of snort that may have been a snicker. "I have a feeling we may need her."

20

Hawk sat at his desk and stared at the clock—3:30. He had an hour and a half till he was to hook up with Cassy. Ninety minutes to do—what? He didn't want to sit here in this sterile workplace and do up his family tree. He'd need a beer or two and the warmth of a pub for that life-threatening assignment.

And there was no point in trying to work on his funding proposals. He couldn't keep his mind on that. For a moment, he found himself missing the comfort of his old, boring job. The template, the predictable questions. For there was nothing predictable about the situation he found himself in now.

What had he hoped to find out from Todd? He'd counted on some inside information on this Peek Society. But he should have known better. All Todd had known was that this was a side business venture with his friend, Vern Warner, and that it had something to do with data derived from caller ID. What were the data to be used for? True to character, Todd had claimed he had no clue.

Hawk shook his head sadly. When it was time to do up Todd's tombstone, he reckoned they'd inscribe it with two words: WHO KNEW?

Well, at least he'd got him to sign a note to the effect that fifty of the video phones had been lent to Hawk, and that those were to be assigned to the Peak Society project.

The other half were Todd's, and he could use them for whatever the "Peek Society" represented.

Todd had looked surprised when Hawk drew up the document and stuck it in front of him with a ballpoint pen.

So, what else could he do? He'd thought about writing up something for the paper from his notes on negative technology. Maybe a guest column or an op-ed piece. But Art Branscomb had taken his idea and run with it. It was the sort of public relations coup that would make most people in the field ecstatic, yet it left him a little envious instead. He wondered how he'd have done writing the column.

Finally, he pulled out the notes he'd been doing up on crisis management. As he leafed through his file, it seemed his sources all offered similar advice.

- Try to anticipate potential emergency situations and prepare for them.
- Don't minimize the problem, but don't blow it out of proportion.
- Assemble all the facts and get the full story out as soon as possible.
- Report your own bad news. Face the public and face the facts.

He looked at his notes and then set them aside. Why was he doing this? He had no idea what might happen. But he had a gnawing sense that something was going to go very wrong.

Then he remembered the faxes from Wally's office. Where were they? Oh sure, in his briefcase. He glanced around the office. Now, where had he put that? It was over by the window. As he got up to get it, he looked out and saw Todd. He'd just left the Hermitage and was heading up the street toward the Wynkoop, at a pretty good clip. Hawk picked up Cassy's chart and tossed it in his briefcase along with Wally's faxes. Then he switched off the light and took off running.

Hawk covered the couple of blocks over to the Wynkoop cautiously, staying thirty feet back of Todd. At the entrance to the brew pub, he waited outside for half a minute before walking in.

He stood in the foyer another minute or two, and looked around for Todd. First, the bar—all four sides and twenty-four stools' worth. No sign of him. Then he went back to the dining area, glancing around the tables, into the booths. It was early—not quite four o'clock—and there weren't many imbibers. It didn't take long to determine that Todd was nowhere in sight.

So, where the hell was he? Hawk had just watched him walk in the door.

He headed back up front, and saw a familiar face. It was the wisecracking waitress he'd encountered the other day when he was with Wally. She was cleaning glasses at the bar.

"He's about so tall." Hawk held out his hand, shoulder height. "Blond hair. Light blue shirt and a yellow tie."

She made a show of peering under the bar in all directions. "Sounds yummy," she sighed. "But I can't find him... Wait, how about over there?"

She pointed behind Hawk to a glassed-in dining room beyond the bar. It was a small room, designed for maybe twenty people at a business lunch, an investment seminar, or a club meeting. When the lights were on, anyone in there could be seen clearly, but from inside it was hard to see the bar.

There was a whirlwind of activity in the private dining room, and Todd was in the vortex, flitting around, his flaxen hair flopping. A couple of guys in denim shirts and dungarees were poking at a cluster of four machines and wrestling with wires. The machines were facing four directions outward from the center of the dining table.

From the replica he'd seen at the office, he knew they were video phones. What was Todd doing with them? And down here at the Wynkoop.

Hawk ordered a pint of Dead Red Ale and took a seat at the far end of the bar. He took a long draw of the beer and let himself relax a little. What was he trying to accomplish, spying on his partner? Basically, he had no idea. But he had time to spare. And he had to do something.

He opened his briefcase and took out the sheaf of faxes. With one eye cocked at Todd, he started through them. The documents were not scintillating reading. They were pretty cold and lifeless, typical office stuff. But something in them caught his attention. He smiled as he thought of Wally. Wasn't there a story in here? Maybe a column. It was a saga of corporate downsizing and of one man's valiant efforts to survive.

Wally had played the game. That much was certain. Stripped of his staff and left for dead on the arid plains of the unemployed, he'd suddenly been discovered by some higher-ups and resurrected. But they'd assigned him to a different organization in a strange industry: a company that managed hotels.

The memos that had come from The Summit Group were matter-of-fact: the location of his new office, the benefit plan. There were no specifics on the work he was to do. Only that he was to provide "technical support" for a product launch. The launch of two products, actually. It seemed that both had been scheduled for September 30. And that was tonight!

Suddenly he saw why Todd was down at the Wynkoop with the video phones. He was setting them up for a demonstration once the public was aware of the product. But where was the publicity? How would they know to come here?

He kept watching.

Hawk finished the last of the faxes and glanced over at the dining room as he was filing them back in his briefcase. He was just in time to see Todd leave the room. He'd left the door open and the lights on.

As soon as he left, the two technicians gathered up their tools and headed for the bar. As they came his way, Hawk got a closer look at them. He noticed that their denim shirts were identical, with a monogram from a temporary employment agency above the pocket.

READY TECH it read, with a logo of a computer monitor and their names in script just below it. One of them read "Grant," the other "Bud." The techs climbed onto two stools next to Hawk and slumped onto the bar. They waved to the waitress and ordered Railyard Ales.

Hawk watched the guy next to him drain half the pint glass with a single swallow. Then the fellow turned to his co-worker. "He said he'll be back in ten or fifteen minutes."

"Is that a promise or a threat?"

"Yeah, I know, Grant," said the other. "I'm beat out, too. What did it take us, two hours to network those four phones?"

"Make it three," Grant grunted. "It's just that guys like that have no idea." He took a generous draw from his own glass, followed by a rumbling belch.

The waitress tending bar looked up. "What's this, an early avalanche? Hey, guys, it's only September."

Bud turned to his friend. "What do you mean? How long it takes to set things up?" Bud asked.

"How long it takes to get an invention to work right. Just think of all those years we put in for Wally, creating this contraption. Then overnight we get laid off, uninstalled.

Programming career goes up in smoke. The next week, somebody up there decides he likes these video phones. Now it's a product with potential."

"Well, at least it's a job," Bud pointed out. "It sure didn't take long till we got hired back as temps. And you gotta admit, this Vern Warner's a decent guy to work for."

Grant muttered, "So was Wally. Remember Gladys, the Office Mom? And the cinnamon rolls?"

Bud quaffed some more beer and laughed sadly. "You know the guy we really have to thank for all of this."

"Sure, Granger Rowe," Grant grumbled. "He's playing us like a steel guitar."

"But he gets what he wants," Bud said. "Did I ever tell you what happened when he was down at the Summit Group? Head of marketing, I guess. My sister's kid, Candy—she took off from college, spent a winter working up at one of their resorts. Ski instructor, that's what they called her. But Candy's a cute kid, and it turned out they had another job in mind."

"Doin' what?" Grant asked. He held up two fingers, and the waitress refilled their glasses.

"You boys gonna need a ride home?" she asked. "Or are you just gonna float out of here?"

Bud took another swig. "Well..." He lowered his voice. Hawk leaned his way to hear him. "They were making porno movies in-house: some gang bang, chick-on-chick thing. At first, she tells 'em she didn't want to do it."

"So?"

"So, they found ways to persuade her. Like cutting her hours on the ski slope. Then cutting off the heat in her cabin. Dead of winter, forty below."

"Yeah, that's the kind of thing I'm hearing around Telwest," Grant agreed. "He gets what he wants, that Granger Rowe."

There was a sudden ruckus at the door, and the Ready Tech men jumped up to open it. Todd stumbled in, carrying one end of the four-foot video phone replica. The man lugging the other half was red-faced and middle-aged. He wore a white shirt and a blue tie—standard fare for a Telwest manager—and a badge with the number 5. Hawk thought back to the Telwest workers in the elevator. He'd seen a 4 or two, but never a 5. This guy was a honcho.

The technicians took over the replica and carried it across the brew pub. They set it down outside the dining room. Todd took the red-faced man by the elbow and showed him the display inside. The manager clapped him on the back and threw an arm around his shoulder. Then he turned to the technicians with a wide smile and motioned them back to the bar.

"Yep, there's one hell of a guy," Bud declared as he clambered back onto his barstool.

"But that may not be enough," Grant said. "CIO: Chief Information Officer. In Vern Warner's case, they say it stands for: 'Career Is Over.' You know how long those guys last in a job like that? Less than three years. That's the average."

Bud shook his head. "There's no telling how long Vern Warner's got, from what I hear. He's six months from the full retirement plan, and you know that's when they try to axe these guys. That's why he had to come up with something."

He leaned toward Grant and lowered his voice once more. "So just what are these guys doing?"

Hawk hunkered down again, to pick up what he could. It was tough. The bar was filling up, just past 4:30. But from what he could gather, Vern had been scouting out ways to use the caller ID data for some time. Like every phone company, Telwest was awash in amazing amounts of data on who called whom. Businesses with caller ID had specific data focused on their customers.

Grant said they called it NAP data: name, address, and phone.

"But what good is that to the phone company?" Bud asked. "I mean, how does that benefit Telwest?"

Grant said, "That's the problem, exactly. The way I've heard it, Warner has been getting into data warehousing—storing all this info on who calls in for what. But he's been waiting for some kind of application."

Straining to hear, Hawk stumbled over some of the technical terminology: NAP data, data warehousing. But he caught the gist of what they were saying. What good is it to know who's buying something if you don't know how to sell them something else?

"So, what's Vern Warner doing?" Bud asked.

"OK," Grant went on, "so he finds out about this video phone of Wally's—not only that, but something Wally's doing with it. You knew about that, didn't you?"

Bud said, "I'd heard rumors. Kind of a private club where they dial each other up and..."

"Exactly. It was just some weird shit Wally got into after his wife took off—or maybe before. Maybe that's why she left him."

"So Vern Warner finds out." Bud took a swig of beer and snorted. "Maybe he dials in one night, eh? For a little action."

"That's about it. He checks out the video phone, fires off a memo to Granger Rowe, and whammo."

"Yeah, but isn't this illegal? And why the rush—why are they trying to pull this off so soon?"

Bud leaned in again as he said this. Hawk squinted at the waitress and nodded at the TV set above the bar where Newt Gingrich was carrying on once again about his contract on America. She grinned and gave a wink as she reached up and turned down the volume.

"Well, as far as rushing this stuff to market, best I can tell is, there's some kind of pressure. End of the quarter and the stocks are down. Investors are restless and somebody's ass is grass. That's what I've been hearing."

Hawk thought about these guys in their denim shirts. Temp workers, to the regulars at Telwest. Who cared what they overheard. Unless you stopped to consider what they already knew—if they'd been working for the company up till then. Well, if he ever needed an inside source at Telwest, he'd be camping at the door of Ready Tech.

"And as far as the legalities," Grant continued, "well, these guys have got the pedal to the metal. They'll set up this side business, work out the technology, and sell out in a flash—before the feds catch on. I mean, those regulators—they've been downsized same as Telwest, right?"

Hawk stared deep into his beer glass. It was a bizarre scenario, but it all hung together. The Peek Society, a product for the folks who are already dialing in on 900 numbers, not knowing that their vital stats are being recorded with every call. Now offer them video phone sex. Talk about value added!

"Besides, they're not going to do it out of Telwest," Grant went on. "They're doing it out at..."

There was a thunderclap of applause as Gingrich wound up his speech at a Republican fundraiser. Hawk missed the doing-it-where part of what Grant said, but he thought he could fill in the blanks.

"The only problem tonight...the technology," Grant was saying. "I mean, there's a question a guy like Warner's got to ask. Not is it new but..."

"Does it work?" Bud added.

Hawk glanced over at the glassed-in dining room where Todd was now seated with Vern Warner. His partner was still a ball of restless energy, wriggling in his chair and bouncing up and down. Vern was nodding silently, his lobster red complexion steadily fading. Whatever concerns

Todd was laying out there, Vern was taking it all in. Hawk had a pretty good idea of what they were discussing.

Finally, the two of them drew their chairs back, and Warner pointed toward the bar. Hawk picked up his briefcase and began turning toward the dining area. But what he heard next stopped him in his tracks.

"Uh oh, here comes that Todd again," Bud groaned.

"Don't sweat it," Grant said. "Those fucking phones are all set up, and they'll probably work if he doesn't trip over the cord. But this guy, Todd, he's not such a bad dude. The word is he's not doing it for the money."

"He's not?"

"They say there's only one reason he's into this."

"What's that?"

"He's looking out for Vern Warner, trying to save his job. He's just trying to help his buddy."

21

As Hawk slowly made his way to the dining area of the brew pub, his head was reeling. So, there was another side to Todd? How could he have missed it? Had he been so focused on his partner's behavior that he'd failed to sense his spirit? Maybe that's what he got from always watching.

Sure, it was a way to stop people from staring at him, by taking stock of them instead. And look at what could happen when he misread people. Like the editor at the paper, the guy with the squint beneath his smile...

But it was time to change all that. There was something he had to find out about someone else in his life, and this time he couldn't merely sit and stare. He stumbled into a booth back in a dark corner. He had a perilous job to do. There was another connection he had to explore.

He grabbed a place mat from a neighboring table. Then he got out Cassy's family tree and slowly began sketching one like it. It took him a few minutes to complete the diagram, sorting out all the uncles and aunts and cousins. But finally he finished and he set out the two charts side by side.

What could he see? Well, at the level of their parents, there was no link. So they weren't first cousins. Then he went to their grandparents' generation. And there it was. His grandfather and Cassy's grandmother had been cousins.

So, what did that make them? Basically, nothing. They had very few genes in common. What they shared were the bonds of a tribe that tried to embrace every member in a kind of extended family, to include every person possible. Their ties were bonds of spirit.

As the thought sank in, he felt as though a lead overcoat had been lifted from his shoulders. With a silent whoop, he slipped his family tree chart in the envelope along with hers. Then he stood up and planted the ball of his left foot on the barroom floor as he spun around a few times with the other. It was a Nanticoke victory dance—invented on the spot—and it drew a round of cheers from the other patrons.

When he sat back down, he drained his glass and, that fast, the waitress appeared with another. "A dance like that, it's on the house," she told him.

From somewhere in the back of his mind, Hawk wondered if his feelings toward Cassy would be so clear, once the alcohol wore off. Those memories of her as a girl were deeply embedded. But the chart was a start. That he could be sure of. He glanced at the television. It was two minutes to five, and someone had switched channels to pick up the news. "Live at Five," an announcer entoned. "The Peak Society and the video phone. It's the next big thing in technology. Join us!"

Something in the hackneyed tagline hit him like a 300-pound nose tackle. He thought about Cassy, grinding out those sales calls. Todd, helping Vern Warner hang on. Teresa, as a single parent, trying to make a living for herself and her son. Join the news team? My God, he should join them all!

There was a fanfare of trumpets from the TV set, and the news anchor came on. "Tonight, we have a special lead story. A new era in technology!" He faded from the screen. And Cassy appeared, in living color. "Hello," she said, "My name's Cassandra Harmon. I'm here on behalf of the Peak Society. Have you heard about the video phone? I'd like you to know about it."

There was a stirring at the bar as the camera panned to a full screen shot of a video phone. Then that picture peeled away to reveal an even more remarkable image. There was a woman seated at the edge of a bed. She was middle-aged and graying, but Hawk could see she still had a decent figure. In fact, he could see it very well. She was wearing nothing but her underwear.

The woman leaned into the camera. "Hello," she said, in a soothing tone. "I'm Gladys, and have you heard about the next big thing? Well, I've heard about your big thing. With the video phone, now you can show me!

"And, do I have some things to show you!" A roar went up from the Wynkoop faithful as she reached both hands behind her back to unhook her bra. Then she dropped her brassiere as she rose from the bed and presented two substantial breasts to the camera.

There was a clamor in the brew pub at the image of Gladys, then a groan of disappointment. "Hey, what the hell?" "That's not the same broad!" The screen went dark and for an instant, a cry of protest erupted. But soon the cries became moans of resignation. "Aw, who gives a shit? That woman's as old as my mother." In a moment, the broadcast resumed with a car commercial.

Hawk peered at the television. What could have happened? Was it sabotage or just a malfunction? And what about Cassy? How had she got on the screen? In fact, come to think of it, where was she?

He sat with his beer and, when the waitress came by, he waved off another. When she made some joke about the television program, he only smiled. And shuddered. After a few minutes, he got up and grabbed a handful of peanuts from the bar. He paced around as he devoured them, cracking shells and throwing them all over the floor. What should he do? Where was she?

It wasn't like Cassy to go on the air and pitch some

product, especially as an opening act for a sad-ass strip show like that. Had she been forced to do it? Or had someone taped her without her knowledge? The possibilities seemed limitless. Now what to do? He cursed himself for not carrying a cell phone. Suppose she was trying to get in touch with him.

Talk about yesterday's technology. All he could do was try the answering machine at home. He picked up the phone on the bar.

There were two messages. One was short, frantic, and aborted. "Hawk, this is Cassy. I'm down at..." At that, the line went dead.

The other message was plenty long—a tirade from Art Branscomb. "Hawk, what the fuck? Here I am over at the editor's house. Had me over for drinks, he was so glad we scooped the TV stations for once: my column in the afternoon edition, negative tech and all that.

"Well, I'll say this is negative tech! First that bimbo on the TV news. Then, the editor dials up the Peak Society on his video phone, and she's back! 'How big is your big thing?' and all that. Proposing all kinds of strange sex acts. And calling him by name! The kids are right here in the room, and the wife of course..."

Hawk hung up the phone. Nothing he could do about that one.

But Cassy had sounded unnerved, and now he was, too. Damn, if he'd only had a cell phone, or a pager. He sat down again and stared into his beer. The froth was gone, and he peered into the dark, red liquid. In time, he felt his mind relax. There was a glimmer in the ale and he gave that his attention. He concentrated on nothing but the light.

He knew why he avoided cell phones and pagers, the tangles of technology. He didn't need to be on call. What he needed was some space to find the spirit of the person he was trying to reach.

"I'm down at..." Someplace south. Must be something in the Denver Tech Center. So, what was down there? Not Telwest, but the Summit Group? He leafed through the file of faxes till he found one that had told Wally where to report. Got their address. He noticed who had sent it: "Granger Rowe." But not with Telwest—at the Summit Group. Hawk snatched up the faxes and stuffed them in his briefcase. He left five dollars on the table for his beer, another five for the waitress who'd brought the free one. He headed out for his car.

As he passed by the bar, he noticed a brown uniform cap, from a delivery service. The barstool in front of it was vacant; guy must be in the men's room. He remembered that he kept a parka of about the same color in the trunk of his car. He grabbed the cap. Then he reached in his wallet, took out two twenties, and dropped them on the bar. Hawk pointed to the bills and to the cap, as the waitress turned his way. She made a show of blinding her eyes and he hustled out the door.

Outside, he tried on the cap. It was a decent fit.

22

Cassy found herself in a small room that had a stand-up wardrobe at the far end of it. The room was dimly lit, but there was a window on one side that looked out on what appeared to be the control booth for a broadcast studio. On another wall was a bright television monitor, showing the studio itself. She recognized the suite of office furniture. So that was where she'd been ushered in to interview Granger Rowe, into a television studio.

That explained the floodlights, but not what she was doing here. Allison had grasped her by the elbow and at once she'd pulled away. For a minute she'd stood there with a clenched fist, staring at the woman and her stuck-on smile. What the hell was this? No one jerked her around like that.

But suddenly the frustrations of her day welled up and washed over her. Eight sales calls and no one would see her. Not until this Granger.

She'd sucked in her breath and followed Allison through the door, out of the studio and down a hallway. Then another door and Allison held it open with a welcoming smile. "If you'll wait here for a moment..."

And then she was gone.

Cassy quickly tried the door; it was locked. Then she'd looked around and found the telephone. She'd started to leave a message for Hawk and heard the line go dead.

It wasn't like her to panic, but now she was scared. And

mad. How could she have been so dumb! But after a few minutes, she began to settle down. It wasn't altogether bad, sitting in the semidarkness. It gave her time to envision what might happen when the door opened—who might be there, how the hell she could get away. Even where she might try to hide if they came after her.

Suddenly there was a flurry of activity in the control room. Cassy stepped over to the window and peered inside. At the far end of the booth, she spotted a familiar character. Wally was sitting at the edge of his chair, leaning into a computer keyboard. He seemed in perpetual motion as he worked rapid-fire, shaking all over and stabbing at the keys. In the doorway stood the rotund figure of Granger Rowe, the interviewer she'd just met. He was waving his arms at Wally.

Cassy watched the pantomime, wishing she could hear what was being said. Then she noticed a knob beneath the window. A small sign said: Control Room. She turned the dial and a tirade erupted, filling the room.

"What do you mean it doesn't work? You can't separate the 'key fields'? What the fuck does that mean?" Granger roared. "How the hell could you have mixed up those data bases?"

She could hear only snatches of the responses Wally was croaking out in a weak, constricted voice: "... let go all my staff... not used to doing..."

"Well, you've got to—that's why I kept you on," Granger shouted. "You're the tech support guy, right? It says so on your contract. So, what are we going to do? Every time one of the Peak Society members dials into his address book, he gets an eyeful of this—from the Peek Society." He gestured angrily toward the TV studio.

Cassy saw a splash of color on the TV monitor, and an undulating form. Gladys was standing by the bedside, clutching herself beneath her kimono as she slowly lay back and let the garment fall away. There was no question as to what she was doing. And she was moaning the name of a bank president as she was doing it, something or other about his "big thing."

Again, there was a roar from the control room. "Well, if you can't stop transmitting that shit, at least we can do something about the content. Where did you come up with that woman?"

Wally mumbled something.

"Office Mom. What the fuck is that? I mean, you call that woman a sex object? Why, she could be my mother."

Wally muttered a reply.

"What do you mean, save her job?" Granger thundered. "What kind of reasoning is that?"

He swung around in Cassy's direction, toward the hall. "Allison, come in here!"

Cassy drew away from the window, back into the shadows. He called again. "All right, Allison, *please* come here."

Cassy watched the long, lean redhead she'd just met step slowly into the control room. Granger gave her an aggrieved smile and stroked his chin. Cassy leaned toward the speaker. It appeared he was about to say something of importance. But, just then, the door opened behind her on the far side of the dressing room, and Gladys came in. She was walking slowly, in a dispirited sort of shuffle. Cassy did a double take, for the image of the very same woman was twisting and moaning on the television screen, and wearing the same kimono.

The woman gave a sad laugh as she saw Cassy gaping at her. "Just re-runs of the same tape," she said. "They had me voice-over every one of those Peek Society guys by name. 'Charlie, lemme see yours.' 'Frank, I hear you got a big one.' A hundred times like that. Peek Society's got a big membership."

Cassy introduced herself before she turned back to the Granger and Allison show. She'd missed his opening lines, but soon caught the substance of the episode. Allison was turning red, her complexion approaching her hair color.

"You want me to do what?" she was hissing. "You want me to do that? On camera?"

"Look, Allison. What are we going to do?"

"Well, I'll tell you something you should not have done: schedule two product launches on the same night, with an untested technology." Her eyes were on fire.

Granger found an empty space on a credenza in the control room. He leaned back and scrunched his head into his collar, braced himself as though waiting for her to strike him. Then, slowly, he looked up, assessed her mood, and began speaking in a low tone that steadily gained volume.

"Think about it—do you really believe they brought us here to fit into their system? You think they want another guy in a white shirt and a blue tie the color of their logo?

"Allison, you know what's going on. These guys are frantic for something to sell. That's why we're here, and they don't know that much about us. We've gotta make some noise. And this video phone? This is huge. The first real product they've come up with in two years. And just in time to save the quarter!"

Allison stood very still and looked at him in silence.

"Okay, about the two product launches...you remember that Vern Warner, the CIO guy? You know how many subscribers he's got for the phone sex thing? Well, he let it slip about the product launch. Told 'em it was tonight. Told 'em if they tuned in, they were gonna see some action."

Allison took a step toward him. Her eyes were blazing.

Granger collapsed back against the credenza. "So how the hell was I supposed to know how many of these Peak Society guys were also in the phone sex group? Plus, who'd have guessed that Wally fucking Houdini, here, couldn't even keep two data bases straight?"

Cassy watched Wally Arneson slump down and look away. She was feeling terrible for him. Then she heard a low voice, behind her.

"You know it wasn't always this way. Not for Wally and me."

She turned back to Gladys who had hung up her kimono and was fastening her bra. "I had a career, and he did, too. You know, I was once the top-rated stenographer at the phone company. They had contests in shorthand, taking dictation, and I always won."

"And I suppose that was when they came out with recorders for dictation, and word processing," Cassy said softly. "And that was the end of shorthand."

Gladys nodded. "But by that time, I'd met Wally. He was a whiz at programming the kinds of computers they had back then. I was his secretary, and we were a team—just like those two, at least till now. And, let me tell you, if they want to survive, they'd better get past this."

"Survive as a couple?" Cassy asked. She thought about herself and Hawk. Was that what they were? A couple?

"Survive on the job, that's what I mean," Gladys answered, wheezing. She was bending over, putting on her shoes, and Cassy thought she looked beat. A full evening of auto-eroticism could be exhausting.

"That's what you learn in an outfit like Telwest—always letting people go. The folks that last, they do it in bunches: in couples, small departments."

"Like tribes," Cassy heard herself saying.

"Like that team of programmers Wally had," Gladys responded, in a halting voice. She headed for the door as she put on her coat and began pounding on it. "Like Wally and me."

Cassy went over and gave her a strong hug. Then she returned to the window on the control room. Granger was shouting again. "Okay, then, where's that other girl? The one who made the sales pitch. She's an intern for Telwest, isn't she?

"She's still in the building? Well, I want to see her contract. There should be a clause in it: 'and other duties as required.' Allison, get me her contract! All right, Allison: *please* get me her contract—now!"

23

Hawk was halfway to the Tech Center when the traffic on the interstate suddenly snarled. Before long, the freeway was a parking lot. He felt his muscles tighten and his stomach turn as he tried to picture Cassy—where, and doing what? Why did she need him? What could he do?

He reached for the radio dial. Tried to get an update on traffic conditions. How long would this fucking tie-up last? But he caught himself in time and pulled back. What could he do about any of that? He settled into the rhythm of the windshield wipers—whap, whap, whap, whap—and tried to envision the place he was heading. A hotel chain in the entertainment business. Broadcasting sports, and motion pictures into hotel rooms. Soft porn productions. And now they were into... phone sex?

It was the new e-conomy, all right. Where everything came down to selling experiences. Bottom line. Now the only way to add value was to intensify the experience. Take the simple joys of phone sex. You upgrade that. Now it's whacking off in tandem over a high-speed phone line, on a monitor. WHAP/WHAP, WHAP/WHAP. He pictured them, in rhythm to the wipers...

The images of sex drew him back to thoughts of Cassy. They were warm thoughts. He knew he loved her more than ever. And yet, there was something about his part in her life that made him feel...

He lowered the window and stuck his head out into

the auto exhaust that was crystalizing in the cold night air. Damn! Would he ever get out of this?

He couldn't see what was blocking the freeway. But there was nothing to do. He closed his eyes to slow his breathing. Tried it and failed, the worries returning. He tried it again. And slowly the reality of the freeway faded. It seemed she was there in the car...

"It's not just the fear that we were closely related," he told her.

"Hey, Cuz," she seemed to say. "I thought we just took care of that."

"No, Cassy, it's not that. It's more about our ages."

She laughed. "So if it isn't incest, what are you so scared of—child molestation?"

"Goddamn it, be serious, Cassy. No, it's something about..."

Suddenly, the traffic started moving. Her image disappeared, but not the conversation. So, what was it that made him uneasy if he had to go in there? What was he afraid of? Was it himself?

A horn sounded behind him and he came back on task. "If he had to get in there..." Of course he had to. Cassy was in that building! What could he do to get inside? The traffic slowed again and he had more time to think of a plan. By the time he turned off the on exit at Yosemite, he had one.

Cassy knew she had only a few minutes to think her way out of a game in which she'd been dealt a very bad hand. At a rational level, she understood this strange Granger couldn't force her into a job role as the successor to Gladys. But Granger wasn't rational; he seemed to be in panic. Plus, she could tell the man was in a position of some power. And, on top of all that, she was locked here in this dressing room—physically trapped.

Gladys was still pounding on the door.

In a moment, it swung open, and Allison was there. She bore a couple of documents and a worried look on her face. As she stepped inside, she took a deep breath.

"Gladys, we want to thank you," Allison sighed. "That's all I can say: we just want to thank you so much." She reached out with one arm to give the matronly performer a warm hug. With her other hand, she gave her one of the papers.

Gladys looked at the official looking form and turned ashen. It was a document she'd seen too often. "Oh, no," she gasped. "After all I... And what about Wally?"

For a moment, she simply stood and swayed in the wake of the news. Then she snatched up her purse and bolted from the room.

Allison took another deep breath and turned slowly back toward Cassy with a purposeful smile. She held another sheet of paper in her hand.

"Ms. Harmon—'Cassandra,' may I call you that? By the way, I'm Allison. Or, Allie—my friends all call me Allie. Do you have a nickname? What do your friends call you?"

Cassy offered a malevolent stare.

"Well, whatever. If I may, I'll call you Cassandra. Because, you know, we're so much alike—how young we are, our professionalism. I sensed that just as soon as you stepped in the door. I thought: why, there is a woman just like me. Of my class and caliber. Given time, I just knew that we would become friends."

"Of your class and caliber," Cassy repeated, with a scant smile. She needed time to think. How the hell could she get out of here?

"Why, yes," Allison responded, beaming. "Of course, given time... and that's what I'm afraid we're lacking."

She went on to describe the video phone program for the Peek Society, and the good work Gladys had done. "We needed a pilot program, of course, and fortunately Wally and Gladys had prepped the system." She gave a tittering laugh. "Although at this point we wish they had piloted it some more."

Cassy watched her performance with feigned interest, one eye on the door. She'd keep an ear out for Granger. Could she handle him one on one? She thought so. A chop behind the ear, a knee to the nuts. Again, she smiled.

"Now, I don't know how you feel about this enterprise we've inherited. By 'we,' of course, I mean Telwest. You know, we can't do this in the open. But the Summit Group... it fits just fine. And there's revenue in it for all of us. I mean, *all* of us." She nodded meaningfully at Cassy.

"At first, you know, I blanched at the thought of this," she went on. "I mean, it's nothing unnatural, you know... just doing for others what most of us do for ourselves 'most every night." She gave another titter, and Cassy smiled.

"And, for so many of our members—the Peek Society, I mean—why for so many, I'll tell you it's a Godsend. The people who are so committed to their careers, and might struggle a bit with other kinds of commitments. Good people, but just not into lasting relationships. I'm sure you know the type I mean."

Cassy nodded. She thought about Gladys's comments—how the survivors had partners, in small groups, as couples. She wondered how this couple would do, how Allison would last without Granger, if it came to that.

After a long preamble, Allison finally cut to the chase. Would Cassy be willing to give this a try? It was, after all, within the terms of her contract when she'd signed on at Telwest—to help out as needed. And did they ever need her now! As a matter of fact, right now. Within the half-hour.

Cassy listened for the footsteps. She turned aside, as though pondering the request, and glanced into the control room. Granger was sitting in a folding chair, at the edge of the room, his back to Wally. He was wiping his brow, and appeared to be exhausted. Maybe she could take him, if she could keep Allison talking till he ran out of patience and came to intervene. But then she had another idea.

"Allie, I've been in this room a long time. Could we get some air in here?"

At the sound of her nickname, Allison melted. She opened the door a few inches, but blocked it with her body.

"Well, there are a couple of considerations," Cassy responded. "One is that I'd want to be paid union scale—the going rate for a television performer. You'd have to add that to the contract."

Allison nodded. She braced the internship contract she'd brought in on the back of her hand, and wrote a few words on it. "Done," she announced. "And the other thing?"

"Oh, just a girl thing," Cassy offered, lightly. "You know that kimono Gladys was wearing? The red one? I don't think it's right for me. You know, for my coloring. Maybe I could go in that wardrobe and look for another."

She smiled at Allison. "And perhaps you could give me a hand."

24

In the parking lot back of the Summit building, Hawk flipped open the trunk of his car and pulled out the parka he always carried in case of mishaps in the mountains. Even when new, the big, brown coat had never made a fashion statement. Now it was worn at the cuffs and the collar, and could have used a good dry cleaning. But it was more or less the color of the cap he'd purloined at the Wynkoop.

Hawk zipped it up, grabbed the cap, and picked up his briefcase as a package to be delivered. Most companies hired retiree-types as security guards on the night shift, so his outfit didn't have to be a perfect uniform. He wasn't expecting to run up against anybody with good eyesight.

He stepped up to the service entrance and rang the buzzer. No response. Hawk turned up his collar against the chilly wind. After a couple of minutes, he rang again. Finally, a door opened, halfway down a long hall, and a squat, stocky figure emerged. The man was outfitted in the dull, gray uniform of an in-house security guard. A nondescript figure, reluctantly roused from his TV set, moving slowly down the hall. But when he was fifteen feet away, the figure suddenly clicked into focus.

Oh, God, it was Sol—the mover he'd met in Wally's office. The guy who'd mistaken him for an attorney, at least for a while.

Hawk scrunched down into his big coat and pulled the cap over his eyes. He ran through a list of ethnic accents, and rejected the Hispanic. That would be Sol's own tribe. He settled once again on a black dialect, but this time from the deep South. And he'd have to add another ingredient to the disguise.

Sol stepped up to a speaker phone next to the door. "Yuh?" he mumbled.

Hawk said, "Package, heah fo'... " He looked down at the briefcase. "Sez Mistuh Granger Rauw."

Sol shook his head. "That's 'Rowe,'" he said, and buzzed him in.

Hawk looked down at the form to sign in. He gave the first name that came to his mind: an old coach. Had he been asked for an ID, there'd have been trouble, but Sol seemed anxious to get back to his television program. He looked at his watch and filled in the time.

"And Mistuh Rauw is...?"

"The name's Rowe—just like your boat, *amigo*. And he's downstairs in the broadcast studio in the basement. All the way down the hall and take the elevator downstairs. Press 'B,'" he added, for good measure.

Hawk nodded thanks and set off down the hall, slightly dragging his left foot as he shuffled. The combination of the accent, if he'd got it right, and the strange gait ought to throw the lummox off his scent. But he wished he'd had a chance to practice the left-foot exercise. There were times when it felt inconsistent.

When he reached the elevator at the end of the hall, Hawk pushed the down button. In a two-story building, he had a fifty percent chance of making the right choice. Keeping his head low, he glanced back at Sol. Uh oh. The man was staring back at him. Should he wave an *adios*? He thought not. At least he wasn't headed this way. Not yet, anyhow.

The elevator arrived and the doors opened. He hustled inside, forgot to drag his foot—damn!—mashed the down button. It was a short trip to the basement. But now what? Which direction?

He stood for a moment, listening for an indication, and it wasn't long in coming. There were muffled cries—a fuzzy "help!"—somewhere off to his right, down the basement hall, and he took off that direction. Along the way, he wondered about his disguise. Would it work again, with whomever he was about to run up against? He decided not.

When he passed a broom closet, he opened the door and tossed the coat and cap inside. Now he was Hawk Kidree again. In business suit, with briefcase. But, what the hell was he doing here? As he raced down the corridor, he was aware he hadn't thought that out.

He ran in the direction of the woman's cries. Was it Cassy? Where did they have her? What were they doing to her in there? There was a short hallway off to the right, and he headed that way until he came to a door marked Dressing Room. That was where he heard the cries for help.

He stopped to listen. No, it wasn't Cassy. Some strange voice was hollering, "Damn it, let me out of here. That bitch! Get me out!" Hawk took a moment to straighten his tie and pat down his hair.

So, why was he here? He still didn't know. But, from the sound of things, that might not be the first item on the agenda.

The doorknob turned, and he went in to find a twelve by fifteen room with a big window on the far side. To his right was a wardrobe that took up the entire wall. There was screaming and pounding inside. Someone had propped a side chair against the door latch on the wardrobe, and he kicked it free. Then he undid the latch, and the door swung open.

A tall, slender redhead tumbled out at his feet. She was gasping for air, and not in good spirits. "That fucking

...What was her name? Cassandra! 'Maybe you could *help* me,' she says... shoves me... When we find her..."

She knelt on the floor, on all fours, until she began to breathe normally. Then she slowly pulled herself up and straddled the side chair. She gazed up at Hawk, wide-eyed. "Oh, my heavens, thank you! Thank you so much. Thank you."

She straightened her hair and held out her hand. "I'm Allison."

Hawk thought a moment. He still had no script or alter ego. Well, when in doubt, there was always the truth. "I'm Hawk," he said. "Hawk Kidree, with Mile High Communications. We're in public relations."

Allison looked him up and down and a faint smile began to gather at the corners of her mouth. "I don't know if you're aware of what we're doing here—I suppose not. But this could be providential...

"First things first, however. Is there some way I can help you?" Suddenly she seemed utterly composed—as though she had a role in a play and the script now called for action. "I'm not sure why you're here," she added.

Hawk scrolled through a mental data base of things he might be helped with, and came up blank. But he knew he needed time to orient himself to whatever was going on down here—to figure out where he might begin to look for Cassy. He remembered that he was carrying one prop: the briefcase. He said, "I have some papers to be signed—by whoever's in charge."

"Certainly," said Allison, smoothing her skirt as she got up from the chair. For the first time, he noticed that she was holding a kimono in her right hand. It was turquoise: one of Cassy's favorite colors.

"Would you mind waiting in here, while I locate Mr. Rowe? By the way, I'm his assistant. And I have a feeling he will be most interested in meeting you." She smiled again. "I'll also want to tell him how we met."

Hawk stifled an impulse to ask about Cassy. But this was no time to blow his cover. Instead, he asked if he might use the telephone. Allison picked it up and found the line dead. She said she'd activate it as she went out the door, with a toss of her head and a quick swipe at the wrinkles in her skirt.

In a few seconds, a dial tone came on. Hawk called his home number. There were two more messages, one from Jim Gibbs: General Manager of KGO, the folks who brought you Live at Five. Hawk knew that Jim sometimes went hunting with Todd. In his message, he sounded as though that was what he'd rather be doing.

But in fact it seemed he was still at work, trying to track down any available information on what had gone wrong with the video phones on the five o'clock news show. He left a number and asked Hawk to call him. "It's urgent," he reported. "Urgent!" He said something about making the ten o'clock news.

Hawk felt relieved it wasn't Sports on Six, whose announcer he'd assaulted.

The other call was a new one from Art Branscomb and his message was much the same. His tone had dropped a couple of decibels since the call from his editor's house, and he sounded more conciliatory. He needed info for a follow-up column, badly. Hawk knew he'd want more in-depth info than the TV guy. Should he call a special press conference for print media in the morning?

Or, why not just call Art in, at the same time as the TV station. Give him some kind of exclusive. As for KGO, Hawk looked at his watch; it was 7:30. There was still time to send down a film crew for the late news.

Those were all the messages. Had he expected to hear

more from Cassy? He knew it wouldn't be that easy. God knows where she'd have to call from.

He placed one more call, to Todd's home. The phone rang four or five times, and then a recording came on. "Hi, this is Todd. Can't come to the phone right now. Been called away on a business trip to Nebraska. If this call is urgent, please contact my partner, Hawk Kidree." And he gave Hawk's home number.

Hawk was seething as he put down the phone. Okay, so Todd had unseen virtues, looking out for Vern Warner and all. But that gutless wimp, to check out—run off hunting! He strode across the room to calm down, and found himself facing a window, overlooking what appeared to be the control room of a broadcast studio. Sleek computers and monitors and skeins of wires like spaghetti. And there in the center of the scene was Wally, sitting at a big batch of the equipment. The guy looked white as a ghost as he peered into a black screen with line after cryptic line of computer code.

There was a big, corpulent fellow in a business suit standing right behind him, looking over his shoulder. In a moment, Allison appeared in the control room and took the fat man by an elbow. She twisted him around and started giving him an earful. Hawk started to listen, but he didn't have time for that. He had to make some decisions—fast.

As he stepped back to the phone, he glanced up at a wall-mounted television monitor. There was a broadcast studio with a small set of props at one end. An arrangement of furniture with wood-paneled walls, curtains, and a large bed. He remembered the woman on the television screen. And Cassy.

He dialed up the number at KGO and got Jim Gibbs on the line. In thirty seconds, they made arrangements for the TV crew to come down. Then he called Art Branscomb. The columnist was away from his phone, doubtless pounding out the Rusty Nails, but he left him a message on voice mail.

As he set down the phone, Hawk looked up in time to see Allison and the heavyset man hurrying out of the control room. As soon as they were out of sight, Wally began to look about uncertainly. He was swiveling his head, the way he did when he was nervous, and sweating profusely.

Finally, he fixed his gaze on the doorway to the hall.

He started to get up but then he stopped short, as though he'd forgot something. He opened a drawer beneath the video phone and took out a big, blue badge with yellow letters. He was available for reassignment: "AFR."

Hawk watched Wally fasten the button to the pocket of his shirt as he swiveled in his chair, scanning the control room once more. Then he waggled his head, bolted from the chair, and took off running.

25

Hawk sat for a moment and stewed. What should he do? He felt an impulse to run somewhere and rescue Cassy. But rescue her from what? Run where? And now there was Wally, running amok. Where the hell would he go with his button?

Well, for now there was nothing he could do, but wait. And play out the role...

A single set of footsteps came down the hall toward the dressing room, and Allison opened the door. Now her dress was smooth, her hair unruffled; she looked one hundred percent more composed than before. But, along with her disheveled look, it seemed her warmth had dissipated.

She gave a smug smile and shook her mane of auburn hair. "Hank, Mr. Rowe will see you now," she announced, coolly.

He said, "It's 'Hawk.' So it's 'Mr. Rowe'? Let's make it 'Mr. Kidree.'"

She crinkled her brow as she led him from the dressing room down a hall that ran past the control room to a large television studio. Two circles of light shone in the darkness. In one spotlight, at the far end, was the weird boudoir he'd seen on the TV monitor in the dressing room. And nearby, just inside the entrance, a broad light beamed on an office suite. A large desk sat up on a raised platform. There was a big whiteboard for visual presentations behind the desk, and a couple of side chairs at floor level, a foot or so below.

The fat fellow was seated at the desk in a black Naugahyde chair and he seemed preoccupied, writing something. Allison motioned Hawk to a low-level side chair, from which he found himself peering up at the desk like a supplicant. She took a seat in the other.

So this was Granger Rowe. The architect of Wally's destiny at Telwest. Vice president of something. But now he was ordering Wally around down at the Summit. Hawk stared at the bloated sight of him and felt a wave of rage. It could be this guy had Cassy somewhere. It wouldn't take much to grab his lard ass, throw him up against the wall or off the stage...

But that wasn't the way. He needed to find out as much as he could. He closed his eyes and put his head back into football, playing on the line. You didn't just lunge at an opponent. You had to size him up, see how he carried his weight—find a place to exercise some leverage.

Rowe made a show of proofreading what he had written. Then he looked down from his platform, toward Allison, and nodded.

If he hadn't been watching the two of them from the control room, Hawk might have bought into the scene that began to unfold. But now it seemed their roles were dramatically reversed. Allison looked so subservient, they might have been reading from a script.

She said, "Mr. Rowe, this is the man I spoke of. A Mr. Hank—no, Hawk—Kidree. He has told me he's in public relations."

Rowe gave a condescending smile as he looked down at Hawk. "You know, I've always wondered what that phrase meant. 'Public relations.'"

Hawk paused for a moment. Should he bother with a definition? He looked over his surroundings. To his right was the bedroom setting. To his left, there was Allison, listening politely. 'Assistant, my ass.' He sensed she ran Granger. He wondered if they took turns wielding power. 'You be the bat today, I'll be the ball.' Was that the secret to corporate romance?

Bizarre...

He rose from his chair and, in the same motion, yanked it off the floor, spun it in one hand, and slammed it on the platform by the desk. Then he climbed up to Rowe's level and stood behind it.

"The term is somewhat difficult to define," he said, "but I'll offer an example of what we do. You see, representatives of the media call us when they want to know what's going on. Especially in cases where something's going badly."

Rowe shifted his weight in the big chair. "Can you give an example?"

He nodded to the side chair, but Hawk remained standing. Then he leaned on the desk, looking down at Rowe. "They called me tonight. About five minutes ago. It was KGO, the TV station. The one where your Gladys showed up on the five o'clock news. They wanted to know more about the video phone."

"And you told them?"

"Where to come. Gave them directions. As a matter of fact, they're due here..."

Rowe shuddered. "They're due here? When?"

Hawk glanced at his watch. "In however long it takes to assemble a crew and get through the traffic on the freeway. I'd make it thirty minutes."

"And who gave you authorization to..."

"I'm under contract to Wally. I'm with Mile High Communications. We do public relations. Would you like to go over that part again?"

Rowe was speechless for the moment. He was chalk white.

"Now, let me tell you what to do," Hawk continued. "That's another of our functions. We advise clients what to do under conditions that call for crisis management. And, I believe you'll agree, these sure as shit seem to."

Hawk reached in his briefcase and took out the sheaf of faxes. He pulled out the one from Wally, on the two-month public relations assignment and the signing over of the video phones to Mile High Communications. "The first thing you can do, Rowe, is to write an amendment to this note, giving Wally Arneson lasting rights to the video phone contract for the Peak Society, the civic leaders. He'd signed it over to us temporarily, but he's the one who should own that."

"That jerk? Why, talk about incompetent."

"He's more than that, Rowe, and you know it. You're the one who fired his programmers..."

Rowe sputtered something unintelligible, but he took out his pen. He was glaring at Hawk. "You know, this is my flagship product," he grumbled.

"This isn't your anything," Hawk said. "This isn't even about you. Wally developed that product... And, say, do you know how we're doing on time?"

Allison spoke up. "On the basis of what you told us, we might have twenty-five minutes. That is, if we can believe you."

Hawk ignored her and thrust the fax in front of Granger Rowe. "Now, after you sign, there are two ways to go. You can stay here and tell the television reporters whatever story you can come up with—explaining, by the way, how it was your menopausal porn star saw fit to take it all off on the evening news. And, you can assume that someone will blow your cover down here at the Summit Group. You're a public figure, Rowe. They'll know you're with Telwest.

"Or, you can step out of the spotlight and let me handle this."

Rowe squinted at Hawk, his eyes dark with anger. "And what are you going to do? Put some kind of spin on it?"

"You put a spin on things, it never stops," Hawk muttered. "And maybe that's your problem. What you need to do is spend ten minutes, tell me what's gone on down here. Everything you know. Then I'll be here to stand up to the press."

"And where will I be?"

"That's up to you, Rowe. But I wouldn't rule out the idea of hiding."

The debriefing of Granger Rowe didn't take long. In a few minutes, he spilled everything he knew about the silent partnership between Telwest and the Summit Group. It seemed all he wanted to do was escape the reporters, get back to his office, and contemplate his next big gambit.

In a quavering hand, he signed the amendment to the faxed document.

Hawk suggested they might come up with a project to help out a charity that could use a video phone network. Maybe the refuge for injured wildlife. People who adopted one of the animals could check in with the biologists and see how they were coming along. He remembered that basic principle of crisis management: in the wake of the crisis, do a good deed.

Rowe grabbed his coat and briefcase and headed for the door. Allison made to go with him, but suddenly Rowe was in her face. He looked more contrite but still plenty intense. "Allison, you can't leave—not right now."

"And why not, Granger? From all appearances, you're going." She paused and fixed him with a frozen stare, till her eyes slowly widened. "Oh, no. We're back to that? You want me to climb up on that bed and..."

"Well, after the reporters leave."

"Oh, Granger, how thoughtful."

"Allison, think of the product. The subscribers. That Vern Warner. His caller ID. Do you realize how many callers that guy had on his phone sex list? All you have to do is appear in costume for the reporters, dressed for the part. It's the best publicity we could hope for."

"And then?"

"Well, the rest of it is just for tonight. Closed circuit. Peek Society. Just for the subscribers. Tomorrow, why, we'll go down to Shotgun Willie's. Hire some topless barhops, after hours. Staffing will not be a problem. Allie, it's my next big thing! It's no time to let this go. We're on to something!"

Allison turned to leave, walking slowly, her face flushed red as the third quarter Telwest earnings report.

Hawk watched the interplay, bemused, but he was feeling a little unsettled. Something was stirring in his innards and he knew what it was—the dark spirit of Okee, insidious as ever. But it was playful this time, toying with him. Poking holes in his professional demeanor.

As Allison strode out, he let himself go. "Why don't you go pick out one of those kimonos?" he called after her. "You still have time."

He paused for effect. "And may I suggest the turquoise."

26

Hawk took a deep breath and cleared his head of Allison and Granger, the clangor. He took off down the hall in search of Cassy. As he picked up speed, he caught a flickering image of where she might be. He was racing around the corner, headed for the elevator, when he heard a low grunt—just before a blow like a sledgehammer hit him square between the shoulder blades. Hawk went down in a circus of stars and darkness, smacking his head on the rock-hard linoleum floor.

Somehow, as he lay there, he managed to look up and see who had hit him. It was Sol, the all-purpose thug, standing over him, leering. "Who the fuck are you today? Big shot lawyer. Delivery boy. Take a snooze, asshole."

The human vault turned and started down the corridor for his post at the delivery door. But as Sol took his first steps, Hawk felt something like a fireball building within him. It had a trajectory of its own—rising, gaining momentum. And the figure of Sol became a lineman years ago, in a sweat-stained, purple uniform of Kansas State. Almost unaware, Hawk drew back his right leg and cracked it into the back of the knee of the security guard. Leg-whipped, his cartilage stinging, Sol screamed and seized his leg as he fell to the floor.

Hawk climbed to his feet and stared down at him. He felt a mounting rage— he'd kick the guy's teeth right down his throat—but turned aside. He stumbled down the hall in the direction of—someplace he might find Cassy.

He stabbed at the button for the elevator but stopped in midair. Where the hell was he off to? He needed to collect his thoughts. The image he'd had of where to go had vanished. Halfway down the hall was a door to the men's room. He ran inside and collapsed on the floor. He didn't turn the lights on.

In the darkness, he sat cross-legged and tried to clear his mind of everything outside, to focus on nothing but his breathing. It took a few minutes, but slowly the beat of his breath turned resonant and he felt the throbbing rhythm of the drum. He concentrated on Cassy. As a vision of her began forming, he followed it back in time.

There was an incident when she was small. She'd run away in fear of something. He saw it—the time he'd thrown her out of the basketball game. His stomach began to quiver. He hated this sense of regression, to think of the two of them back then. But he had to go back and try to remember.

Slowly, an image rose and began to take shape. Of course! He had a sense of where to go—or, at least where to begin looking. He started out the door, but stopped in his tracks. Someone was out in the hall. Was it Sol?

He swung the door open with a fist at his side, but he stopped and grinned. Art Branscomb was tottering down the hall, bracing himself against a wall with one hand, a reporter's notebook in the other. Hawk took one look at the ex-psychiatrist and wondered how much he remembered from medical school. With a twinge of guilt, he thought of his assailant, Sol. If the guy could put weight on that knee, he'd be all right. If not, he'd be walking with a limp for the rest of his life.

"Art, I'm glad you made it. Say, there's a guy up ahead there who had an accident."

"Is he part of the story?"

"Well, no. But, you were a doctor, and I think he's..."

"So, is that why you called me down here? Some kind of mission of mercy?" He held up his thin, spiraled notebook. "What's this look like—a first aid kit? Who do you think I am? Mother Theresa? God damn it, Hawk, you owe me. Where the hell's the story?"

Hawk shrugged at his friend and nodded toward the studio. As Branscomb shuffled down the hall, he turned the other way and scanned the corridor. Now, to find her. Where was Cassy?

But there was a rumble in the parking lot. A van pulled up, and then another. There were shouts of where to go, where to send the equipment. The TV crew was here, in full regalia.

Hawk went to the delivery door and ushered them in. With Sol out of commission, there was no problem now with getting past Security. Maybe less danger to Cassy. But where the hell was she?

He met the reporter, a young guy named Rod Roderick. He had spiked hair; energetic, clear, blue eyes; and narrow glasses. Except for the fashion of the day, he might have passed for Todd ten years ago.

"Thirty minutes," Rod declared. "That's what we've got. A half-hour, tops." Hawk led the reporter, a camera operator, and a sound man back to the television studio. The studio was pitch black, except for the two circles of light on the office suite and the bedroom set. Hawk set up shop in the office.

He sat against the edge of the desk and left the reporters on the floor, a foot below the raised platform. He introduced himself as the spokesman for the video phone projects: "I can tell you what I know about what's gone on here."

Rod turned to the camera man: "Roll it." Then he put a hand up. "Whoa! Wasn't there a gal who started out, talking about this on the five o'clock news? Seems like she was cut off. Is she around?"

Hawk shook his head. He said, "Well, I'm afraid..." and then a clear voice came out of the shadows.

"Here I am, right here," Cassy announced, and she climbed up on the platform.

She looked as poised and confident as anyone Hawk could imagine. He felt a chill of excitement and elation.

"That's great," Rod exclaimed, and he took down her name. "Who are you with?" he asked, "and what's your position?"

Hawk touched her arm. "She's with Mile High Communications," he answered. "Account executive for the Peak Society project. That's P-E-A-K. I'm Hawk Kidree, a partner in the firm." He stepped down off the platform.

Cassy gave a brief, but effective presentation, describing the Peak Society as a club for people who had no time for meetings, along with other potential uses of the video phone. As she finished, Hawk noticed Wally had set one up one of the phones on the corner of the desk. He pointed it out to the TV crew, and they filmed it. "So far, so good," he was thinking.

But Rod wasn't through. He stopped the cameras and looked across the studio, at the boudoir. "Okay, now for the bed and all. Isn't that what we saw when that woman took it all off on the five o'clock news? What's up with that?"

Hawk stepped back up to the desk, motioned Cassy off the platform. He felt a sudden instinct to shield and protect her, and the sense of it made him uncomfortable. He turned around and fiddled with the video phone.

"Come on, Kidree," Rod hollered. "We've got maybe fifteen minutes, and the people at the station want to know about this. Not to mention the viewers."

Rod turned to the camera man: "Roll it!"

Facing the camera, Rod's anxious expression melted into a welcoming smile. "Here with me is Hawk Kidree, from the firm that evidently is responsible for the controversial side of the video phone story. Tell us, Mr. Kidree, what are you doing down here with this bedroom?"

Hawk stared wide-eyed at the camera, a deer in the headlights. "Well, it's...," he began, and stopped for a breath.

"Cut!" shouted Roderick. "Look, somebody's gotta come clean and tell us what's been going on down here. You're the spokesman. What the hell's the matter with you? Haven't you ever been on camera before? The word we have is that the whole thing started with Telwest."

"All right," Hawk replied. "I'll give it a shot. But it's a long story and you can't fit it all in a sound bite."

"That's right," echoed a raspy voice from the edge of the platform. "You talk about phone sex, and you've got all kinds of human needs involved. Just like any other form of pornography. Why, in my column tomorrow..."

Rod spun around, wielding his microphone. "Shut up, Branscomb. Nobody reads that shit anyway. What we need here is the punch line. Who's using the video phone for phone sex? Is it Telwest? Or the Summit Group? Who's doing it?"

A deep voice rang out from the doorway to the studio. "I am. It's my thing! And this newscast is just the beginning; we're taking aim at the networks. This is a growth industry we're talking about. It's the future of Denver—the next big..."

"No, Babe. No! You can't afford to come out like that. We can't! Let me tell it." The voice came from next to the bedroom set, as a lithesome redhead slid out of the darkness and slithered up to the head of the bed. As she settled in among the pillows, the kimono she was wearing started slipping off one shoulder.

Hawk watched from the desk set as Roderick and his crew scrambled over to the boudoir. Whatever Granger had started to say was forgotten. "Tits, tots, and pets." The TV guys would follow like lemmings.

"May I have your name?" Rod was looking up at Allison as she rearranged her kimono.

"No, you may not," she snapped, "and I don't want you showing my face. I'll show you as much of the rest of me as you can get away with. But you've got to play what I have to say, verbatim."

"You got that right," Rod agreed. "We're flat out of time for editing. Roll it!"

"All right, assume we're in a new economy," Allison began. "With no more borders between industries. What you're looking at here is a hybrid product. The video phone. It's a link between the telecom space and lodging."

"Between what?" Rod demanded.

"Sure, they're odd partners," she went on, "but they're both in the business of selling experiences. That's the other part of the new economy."

"That's it!" cried the gravely voice again. "Nothing can be sold for what it is anymore. Go to a basketball game, they've got cheerleaders who double as dancers. And if you stay at a hotel..."

"Cut! Shut up, Branscomb. Get him out of here!"

"Look, you idiot, anybody knows what's coming next. They're going to be networking computers, transmitting images night and day. The question is..."

Hawk took Art by the arm and ushered him out of the studio. He didn't put up much resistance. "At least I got my column," he grumbled. "Oh, and that thickset guy in the security uniform? He's okay. He's sitting out there at the door with his leg up. I put some ice on it."

As Hawk came back in the studio, Rod once again yelled, "Roll it."

"For more and more of us these days, a night in a hotel means more than a bed and a shower," Allison continued.

"It's a night away from home." She began to undulate a little. "An excursion into... who knows where? Before it was just over the phone. But, now, with video, it's..."

Suddenly, the platform rumbled as a bulky figure in a business suit leapt up on the bed. Allison drew back in shock.

"I'll tell you what it is," he cried. "It's the next big thing!"

She looked on, aghast, as he thrust himself on camera. She lowered her kimono, offering some cleavage, but Granger now had center stage.

"See, you can't keep selling widgets," he bellowed. "I mean, how many cell phones will one person buy? Now it's all about sports, travel, movies, sex. It's nothing but experiences. That's all you can sell, and you've got to have new ones. That's how you add value. Take the video phone—that's why Telwest..."

"Granger, no!" She shoved him, tried to push him off the bed. "No, Granger. They see this, we'll be... uninstalled!"

Looking back, it was hard to grasp the rest of that night. The whole scene had a sense of unreality. Everything was running at fast forward. And out of scale, as though they were up on a big screen, in Diamondvision. He himself felt larger than life, like the hero in some weird Charlton Heston action flick. Was that what egomaniacs like Granger Rowe did to you?

There was a swirl of lights and cameras, the film crew in a frenzy. Then, in an instant, they were off to make their deadline, racing up the freeway for the ten o'clock news.

Hawk had scanned the room in search of Cassy. But it seemed she, too, had vanished into the night. He felt a moment of panic, an urge to rush off and rescue her again. But it quickly passed, and he wasn't sure why.

As the studio cleared, he watched Allison begrudgingly

trudge toward her performance. There was a flash of bare breast and bright nipple as she climbed up on the bed. But suddenly she turned in his direction with a dark scowl. It was clear he wasn't welcome for the act that was to follow.

He picked up his briefcase and headed out, still in something of a haze. The Allison and Granger show had to be one of the weirdest corporate scenes in town. Maybe it was the modern-day version of an industrial accident. It used to be the classic chemical explosion. Or the machinery on the assembly line running amok. But this was a media-driven disaster. Your career was based on getting noticed, and if you lost control of your image, your resume caught fire and you went down in flames.

As he turned to leave, he caught a glimpse of classy Allison, splayed out on the sheets. He thought he saw her go into a sort of slow motion, and all the way out to his car, his imagination filled in the rest of the routine. The way her back would arch as she touched herself, undulating in her kimono.

At a gut level, he knew he understood the voyeuristic business of video phone sex very well. He felt the sap rising. As he climbed in the car and cranked the ignition, his thoughts returned to Cassy. The need he'd felt to rescue her seemed absurd. It was obvious she didn't need him for that; she could take care of herself.

But he had some needs of his own, and they were mostly carnal.

Hey, it was only ten o'clock. He could head for her apartment—meet her at the door and take her in his arms. Whip out the family tree...

The scene didn't play well. He opted for the Wynkoop, instead.

The waitress hadn't gone off shift. She was standing at the cash register, ringing up a tab and she eyed him as he walked by the bar. "Hey, Champ, back so soon? What's it been—two, three hours? Say, you know, something about you looks different..."

Hawk flashed a puzzled grin.

"Wait, I've got it. This is the first time I have ever seen you smile."

He settled into a back booth and ordered a Churchyard Ale. Along with a pint of Splatz Porter, for good measure. He sat in the darkened brew pub with his frosty, frothing glasses and smiled to himself, savoring the triumphs of the night. He had to admit there was something enticing about a Granger Rowe. Inflating your ego, drawing you into his drama. But, shit—he'd stood him off. He took a long draught of the dark porter, then the ale.

Still, it wasn't long before his thoughts returned to earth, to all the many fragments of his life. How would they reassemble in the morning? So much had changed. Cassy, for one. He felt different about himself, as well. He wondered if the bond they had shared would be broken, without the scintillating drama of suspecting they were cousins. One way or another, he sensed that when they met again, it would be on a wholly different plane.

And it could be that was all he could count on. After everything that had transpired, Denver would look different in the morning. He thought about Wally and felt a surge of hope. Maybe the deal he'd cut for the video phones would reassemble his client's life. Perhaps the two of them would have some work again. And then there was Todd. Ah, Todd. For now, Hawk was sure he had the upper hand in their odd partnership. But for how long?

The beers were beginning to take effect, feeding on his fatigue. He sank back into a corner of the booth, where the woodwork met the brick wall. As he drained the last of the dark, pungent porter, his surroundings began to blur, the brew pub revolving around him.

He found himself fading into the future...

A curtain opened on a new stage and another scene began to take shape. He recognized the setting; it was the hall outside Todd's office. He'd been walking by the office when the door swung open and his partner popped out, saying something though Hawk couldn't make out many of the words. The action was playing out in a herky-jerk motion, like a motion picture film that was missing some of its sprockets.

Todd clapped him on the back and drew him into his office. Hawk noticed the elks' heads on the paneled walls. They were staring down wide-eyed, in amazement. Todd's buddy, Vern Warner, was sitting behind the desk, hunkered down over the phone. His face was flushed and he was breathing hard. He was talking intensely. Hawk tried to pick up the conversation, but it was spotty.

"You want Hawk... represent you? As your agent? Okay... ask him."

Vern wheeled in his chair, dragging on a cigarette. He seemed short of breath, puffing. He turned to Todd as though Hawk wasn't there. "It's Benjie... wants an agent... go over the deal before we show it. Turns out... your partner."

Todd turned to Hawk with that same ingenuous grin, his trademark look of oh-wow wonderment. "So, here's a slot for you, Hawk. Sure, a lot of things... changed. But they always do. The point is... what's next in line."

Todd flicked a switch on the wall, and Hawk heard a familiar voice hollering from the TV monitor behind him. "Shit, man, you was there at the game. You seen it. I done deeked that motha-fucka."

Hawk turned to watch the video, but he knew what was coming. It was a scene he'd witnessed in the Broncos' locker room. "Hey, man, I wasn't thinking. You can't be thinkin' when you deekin.'"

The on-camera guy had walked away with a shrug of

futility as Benjie carried on. This was nothing fit for prime-time viewing. But the video kept rolling. Hawk watched as the young woman reporter walked up. Benjie promptly dropped his towel, but the camera rolled on.

Hawk heard a raspy voice behind him, a salacious laugh. "... hung like a knockwurst... Think the gals... go for it?" Vern asked, rhetorically.

Hawk turned back to Todd who now wore a sheepish grin. "Vern stayed up all night... business plan... How many guys like to take it all off in front of the reporters?... any idea? How much footage is out there?"

Hawk scrutinized his partner. "Full frontal nudity, from locker rooms?"

"Hawk ... It's hot ... ask Vern, here ... market research ... Soft porn for females ... next big thing ... and we're ... ground floor. We're in on it!"

Slowly the image of Todd began to fade and the brew pub came back into focus. Hawk rubbed his eyes and shook his head. He sat for a moment and stared down at the rings left by his beer glasses on the table. When the waitress came back for a refill, he waved her away. For a time, he sat and thought some more. Finally, he got up and headed slowly for the front door.

He was standing at the cash register, when he saw it. The button was big and blue and it had the same familiar letters in bright yellow: AFR. It was lying on a bar towel, next to the beer glasses.

The waitress saw where he was looking as she brought him his change. "Oh, yeah. Talk about a strange tip, hey?"

"I've been seeing a few too many of those around town," Hawk said.

She said, "It was that skinny guy, that geek. Comes in here a lot. That one time, I saw him with you. Well, tonight he walks in, not too steady. Grabs a couple of pints, as though he needed more, and heads over there." She nodded toward the glassed-in room with the video phone display.

"Somebody lets him in and pretty soon he's going at it, punching at the keyboard on one of those crazy phone-with-the-screen things. He's in there maybe twenty minutes, poking at them keys. All the while swilling his beers and pretty soon we can hear him through the glass door. Swearing, hollering. Seems like something wasn't going to his liking."

"When was this?" Hawk asked.

"Maybe five minutes ago. You just missed him. So, he comes reeling out and over to the bar here and he grabs something in his pocket. I think he's bringing out another bill. But it's this thing." She picked up the button.

"He looks at me and his eyes are blank, just empty. Hands over the button, says I might as well have it; he's got no use for it anymore. He starts for the door. I holler, 'Hey, you want a cab?' But when he turns around he gives me that same dead look. Then he's outta here. He was in no shape to be driving."

Hawk ran out the door and into the street. There was no sign of Wally.

He drove slowly down East Colfax in the deep darkness just before dawn. He was cradling a cup of black coffee from an all night drive-in in one hand, balancing a breakfast burrito against the steering wheel in the other. He never had found Wally.

Through half-lidded eyes, he watched a stack of newspapers rustle and then break free in the brisk wind of November, the top sheets fluttering down the dusty street to lodge against a pile of gray detritus. Further on, a vagrant emerged from an alley behind an all-night, adult video store. He was dressed for the dead of winter, all the clothes he owned piled on his back, pushing a shopping cart filled with bottles and aluminum cans.

The ambiance of East Colfax.

Hawk kept the car windows closed as he sipped his coffee and bit into the warm cheese and scrambled egg and bacon of his burrito. Soon enough, he'd be quaffing the stench outside.

Just as he finished the last crumbs of his breakfast, he arrived at his destination. A faint glow of dawn framed the bright red neon sign of Argonaut Liquors. The store did a land office business in this low rent district, converting some of the overhead it saved into discounts for its customers. Hawk knew there was a certain stimulation in visiting Argonaut for most of the regulars. Finding a parking place as close as possible to the entrance, then hustling in to spot the specials of the week before rushing back out to the car with an eye out for one of the store's security guards. If he himself had never experienced that kind of excitement, it was one of the costs of being so big that the vagrants of East Colfax couldn't faze you.

He drove around back and found what he was looking for. Then he parked the car and flipped the trunk open. Nearby, there was a huge mound of cartons for hard liquor, the sturdiest kind, and he found a few that looked just right for hauling files. But as he reached out to snag the first one, he gave a start.

The pile seemed to be moving. First it shuffled on the far side, then gave out with a low, growling sound.

A head popped out with a dark knit cap and a grisly beard. "What the fuck you doin' with my shelter?" The head took stock of Hawk, then drew back below the boxes with a grumble. Hawk looked around at the edge of the mound and saw a shopping cart with the man's few possessions.

"Sorry," he muttered, "I didn't know," and he moved down to the other end of the boxes. In a minute or two, he'd filled his trunk. Now he could clean out his desk, pack up his files. But he'd also filled his head with misgivings. What the hell was he doing? How many months could he hang onto the condo? How many paychecks separated him from a new career in a drive-in on East Colfax? Or from the creature in this cardboard hovel?

He stopped for a moment when he was back in the car, the boxes in his trunk. He sat with his hands gripping the steering wheel. He looked in the rearview mirror and glanced back at the cardboard shack. Then he put the car in gear and turned left onto Colfax. He headed for the office.

27

There was a light snow drifting through the moonlight as they plodded from the depths of the forest on the path back to their car, single file. She was puffing as they unclasped their snowshoes and tossed them in the trunk.

"There are some things you can do in the sixth month." She paused for breath and glanced at him with a glint in her eye. She punched him in the ribs. "Did you know that? There are some things you can still do—but this ain't one of 'em."

He grinned and opened her car door. Made a show of adjusting her seat belt below the swell of her belly. Then they rode along in silence until they drove into the parking lot of the looming stone and timber lodge.

"How are you coming on the column?" she asked as they entered the great room of the lodge.

"I'm far enough along that I can forget about it for tonight... By the way, did I ever tell you what they always say around the newspaper about having a column?"

"Yes, you did, and I don't need to hear it again." She gave him another shot to the ribs, through his parka.

There was a red glow around the lounge from the blazing fireplace. Some hanging lights and small lamps added a warm cast of amber. He had been here before, when his friend, Natalie, had worked here. And he vaguely recalled a dream about this place. Dancing in the round, to the drumming.

They stopped by the fireplace and took in the pungent aroma of burning piñon. Then he turned around and peered through the dim light over toward the bar. They were thirty feet away when he heard the voice he'd been expecting.

"Hawk! Cassy! Got a couple of empty places. Come on this way."

They shed their parkas as they climbed up on the bar stools. Hawk smiled at Art Branscomb and leaned over the bar to hug him. "My God, it's good to see you. And your diploma looks great against that wall. Where'd you get it framed like that?"

Art shrugged. "Did it myself. Got my own shop, you know. Knocked out the frame, finished it, stained it, same shade as the bar. You know how people are always saying a bartender would make a good psychiatrist. All I did was reverse the roles. Here, let me stir you up a couple of Rusty Nails."

They threw up their hands. Cassy was on nonalcoholic sodas; Hawk opted for a microbrew. Art set up their drinks, with a Rusty Nail for himself.

It was a quiet, weekday evening at the resort, and Art had time to visit between pouring the occasional mixed drink and pumping out a draft beer. At times, he'd go down the bar and listen to a patron, nodding now and then, with a pat on the arm.

It was a side of his friend Hawk had seen before, but not in professional practice. "Looks like he's found a way to care about people without being overwhelmed by what's wrong with them," Hawk whispered to Cassy. "Maybe the trick is to listen while you're half-loaded."

Midevening, Art's shift was done, and the three of them decided to have dinner at an open café at one corner of the lounge. "So, how does it feel, not having a column?" Hawk asked when they settled in, after they'd ordered.

"Hey, there's a good line I could lay on you—if we weren't in mixed company."

"Don't let me stop you," muttered Cassy. " I know it by heart. Something about a nymphomaniac."

Art chuckled for a moment, then turned serious. "That was a turning point, that night down there at the Tech Center. I guess it was two years ago, and it seems like yesterday. That night changed our lives, wouldn't you say? Every one of us."

"Was that when you decided to give up the column?" asked Cassy.

"No, but it was when I knew the time was coming. Maybe it was getting myself all riled up with those TV creeps, trying to beat 'em to a story. I should have known it was a lost cause. We can't compete on deadline. Newspapers are for exploring what a story means, not just telling what happened."

"But it's tough to find an audience for that, especially in a run-and-gun place like Denver," Hawk said.

"You bet, and it was time to bring in fresh troops, let a younger guy take that column. By the way, I think you're doing a hell of a job. And, look what happened to you two: married. What is it? Must be over a year now."

Cassy was quiet for a minute before she said, "I think we go back to that night, too," somewhat meditatively. Then she brightened. "That's when Cochise, here, discovered he couldn't rescue me—maybe found he didn't need to." She gave Hawk a kick under the table.

"But I knew where to look," he countered. "The last stall in the men's room in the farthest part of the building. Same kind of place you hid when I threw you out of that basketball game. And don't tell me it didn't cross your mind to go up there and wait for me to find you."

She smiled with a shrug and dipped her head.

"So, Cassy, I hear you're freelancing now," Art said. "And Telwest is one of your clients."

"She's doing great," Hawk interjected. "They were all over her when they saw the kind of presentations she can make. The best part is, she's there on her terms. She can set her own schedule, once the baby comes."

"And what about that crazy client of yours?" Art asked. "Was it 'Harry'"?

"Wally," Hawk said, turning sober. "I guess I've never talked to you about that night, what happened after we left the studio."

He told about going to the Wynkoop, spotting the button on the counter. "I drove around most of that night, down by where he lived, past the Telwest building. Every place I thought he might have run for shelter. It was obvious he was distraught, must have made one final stab at fixing the damn address book on the data bases.

"I knew he was in no shape to be driving. Thought I'd flag him down, get him off the road, then tell him the good news about the video phones. How I'd wrestled them away from Granger Rowe and now he owned the product. He could start over, maybe even hire some programmers."

Hawk stopped and took a deep breath, then a sip of his beer. As he looked up, his eyes were glistening. "They found him some time about three in the morning. Cops had a call from someone at the base of Lookout Mountain. I don't know how the hell he got himself up that winding road in the condition he was in. But he must have had an idea where he was going. It was the road up on the east rim, the one they call Lariat Trail.

"There's a stretch of straightaway clear at the top and it seems he got a good running start before he drove off the side. Some kids were parked up there and they saw it all. It's a straight drop if you go off at the right spot."

"I'd guess he'd rehearsed it," Art said, glumly.

Hawk said, "There wasn't much left when he hit bottom."

Cassy winced at the familiar story. Art sat in silence for a while. Finally, he said, "Even if he'd got it to work right, do you think the video phone would have saved him?"

Hawk sat silent for a moment. "I've thought about that," he said. "One thing we now know, of course, is that the contraption was a lost cause. Along came the Internet and you could have all the video sex you could handle, in the blink of an eye. Pretty soon, I hear, they're going to be transmitting over cell phones."

Cassy shook her head. "It's no wonder they talk about staying ahead of the curve if you want any kind of career. Stay light on your feet." She laughed. "Although that's not me, not these days."

Art looked at her and laughed, then turned somber. "But think of what it costs in human terms to develop one of those high-tech wonders. All the days and nights it takes, just to get one of the damn fool things to function."

Hawk nodded. "Then the next big thing comes down the chute."

"And you're yesterday's news," Art mumbled.

The waitress brought their entrees and they ate without talking. It was quiet in the lodge and they all seemed to resonate with their refuge in the mountains. Hawk found himself gazing toward a vast, red Navajo rug in front of the stone fireplace. It was where he had dreamt of the great circle dance. Of Cassy in her leather and feathers. The dancing, the drumming...

He blinked as Art clapped him on the shoulder. "So, did you hear about that?"

Hawk gave a start. "Huh?"

"What I was just saying, about that Granger Rowe. Up

here selling time-share condominiums. Somebody said they saw that Allison with him."

Hawk shrugged.

"Well, thank God he's out of Denver," Cassy sighed. "After all that, end of story."

"If you can believe that," Hawk mumbled.

Art squinted at him. "And what the hell does that mean?"

"I can translate," Cassy said. "You know, it's Nanticoke theology. Manito, the god who gives life. Okee, who destroys it: the other *hombre* Hawk was always afraid he'd find inside him. You must have heard him on the subject."

Art took a long, slow sip of his drink. "The return of Granger Rowe, eh? In a culture that can't sit still, another incarnation of the same damn spirit. I suppose it's one way to look at things. Maybe it is the spirits that give life to the drama. The rest of us characters are just here to enact it.

"Speaking of which, what about your partner, Todd? You know, all we get is rumors, up here. Did I hear he bought you out? That's perfect for him. Talk about contacts! No worries about king schmoozer."

Hawk nodded. "Not as long as there are pheasants in the Sand Hills of Nebraska. Remember his friend, Vern Warner? The guy made it six more months till he was vested in the retirement program. The next day, of course, he quit Telwest. And died of a heart attack four months later."

The three sat in silence for a long time. Then Cassy pushed back her chair, and looked up at the two of them. "I guess there's one more to account for, and it's Hawk, here. Art, you said that was a decisive night, and for the two of us it really was. It took us some time to sort out who we were and where we were—make sure we wanted to be together. But, looking back, it seems like something happened that one night. Something let him love me."

She laughed. "I can't pass up the chance to put you on

the spot, Babe, what with the resident shrink here. Do you have any idea what happened?"

Hawk said nothing for a long time, looking toward the fireplace. Finally, he spoke. "I suppose I could say I saw you grown up. When you gave your pitch for the video phone on TV, and then I screwed up my part, on camera. You really didn't need my help, and I saw that."

Cassy sighed, "About time... But was that the whole story?" She looked over at Art, inquisitively. "He thought I was helpless? I mean, the dude knew I'd been working in gambling casinos."

The old psychiatrist paused for a moment and eyed the two of them. "Well, Cassy," he said slowly, "I'm not so sure the big fella's problem was ever actually you."

"Really?" She looked genuinely puzzled.

"No, I wonder if it wasn't about something in himself," Art began. "About what might happen if he felt he had to defend you... But that's just conjecture." He looked away and took a swig of his libation. "They always say the patient knows best."

Hawk had been gazing at the fireplace. Now he cocked his head and squinted, as though he'd caught sight of something in the flames. "It was back to those Nanticoke spirits," he said, finally. "You know, Cassy's right. I'd always been afraid of the darkness of Okee—that side of me.

"But, do you remember that last time when I lost my head and leg-whipped the security guard? What was his name, 'Sol'? I mean, he could have torn his ACL, gone around with a limp for the rest of his life. And I left him lying on the floor there.

"Then you came stumbling down the hall." He chuckled. "Drunk as a skunk, weren't you, Branscomb? Hammered like a Rusty Nail. But you came back to check up on him, no matter what you'd said. You cared about that guy. And look at how you helped that poor bastard."

Hawk fell silent again. He looked at Cassy and their unborn child. He said, "I saw that Manito was bigger than me." And he stared off into the fire.

ACKNOWLEDGMENTS

This book is dedicated to two special colleagues whom I lost this year. David Van Meter was a close personal friend who died in May. The author of two major mystery novels, David always took time to coach me in my fledgling efforts to work in this genre. I will always miss his supportive, caring spirit and candor.

Like David, George Stein was a refugee from corporate life. After a long career as a manager of technical communications, George and his wife put down roots in Las Cruces, New Mexico. There, he founded Barbed Wire Press, a publisher of books that dealt mainly with the American West, a region he loved. *Soundings* was to have been published by Barbed Wire, prior to George's untimely death in January.

I appreciate the help of two public relations professionals and friends, Tom Schilling and David Henderson, in helping me understand the methodologies of that field. I relied also on published materials from the Public Relations Societey of America. I am thankful also to Dr. Jerry Harmon, Dean of Education at Eastern New Mexico University, and a former football coach, who taught me (at less than full speed) the mechanics of the leg whip.

The history of Nanticoke Native Americans has been told in many ways. I chose to portray two of the Nanticoke deities, Manito and Okee, as symbols of warring spirits in the universe. The Nanticoke people represent one of many mixed-racial groups found in the United States, principally in the Southeast. The best book I've found on racially hybrid groups in America is *Almost White* by Brewton Berry.

As always in my writing, I am grateful for the personal support and editorial assistance of my wife and friend, Phoebe Lawrence.

Printed in the United States
91580LV00002B/241-258/A